# YEARLING BOOKS

Since 1966, Yearling has been the

leading name in classic and award-winning

literature for young readers.

With a wide variety of titles,

Yearling paperbacks entertain, inspire,

and encourage a love of reading.

# The Five Ancestors

Book 1: Tiger

Book 2: Monkey

Book 3: Snake

Book 4: Crane

THE FIVE ANCESTORS

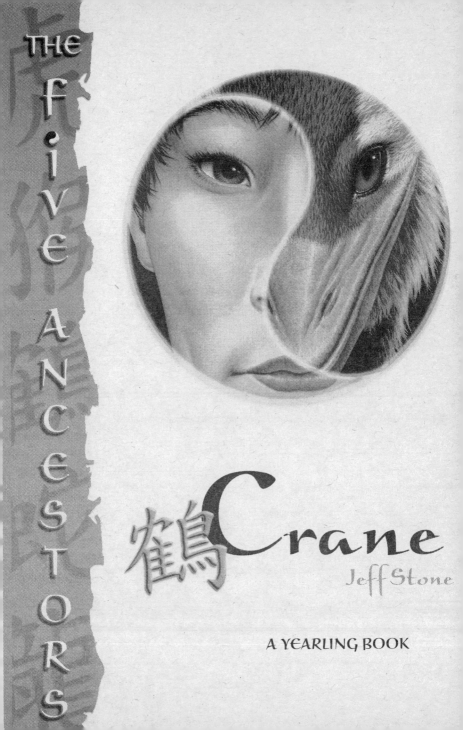

# 鶴 Crane

Jeff Stone

A YEARLING BOOK

*for my mother,*
*Arlene*

Published by Yearling, an imprint of Random House Children's Books
a division of Random House, Inc., NewYork



---

Visit us on the Web! www.randomhouse.com/kids and www.fiveancestors.com

Educators and librarians, for a variety of teaching tools, visit us at www.randomhouse.com/teachers

---

ISBN: 978-0-375-83078-5

Reprinted by arrangement with Random House Books for Young Readers

Printed in the United States of America

February 2008

10

First Yearling Edition

## The Legend unravels . . .

Cangzhen's strong, young Dragon has disappeared and little Monkey has been captured! Now, instead of being chased, the Tiger, the Snake, and the Crane must pursue their enemies to free one monk and find another. Down the Yellow River, the trail leads to a dangerous city and a dark underworld. Unaware that their youngest brother is being used as bait in a ruthless trap, the three rescuers may soon need to be rescued themselves. And of the Dragon? The trail is cold and there is little to learn other than dead ends and rumors. Yet the five must regroup if they are to fulfill their destiny as . . .

the Five Ancestors.

THE FIVE ANCESTORS

# 鶴 Crane

Jeff Stone

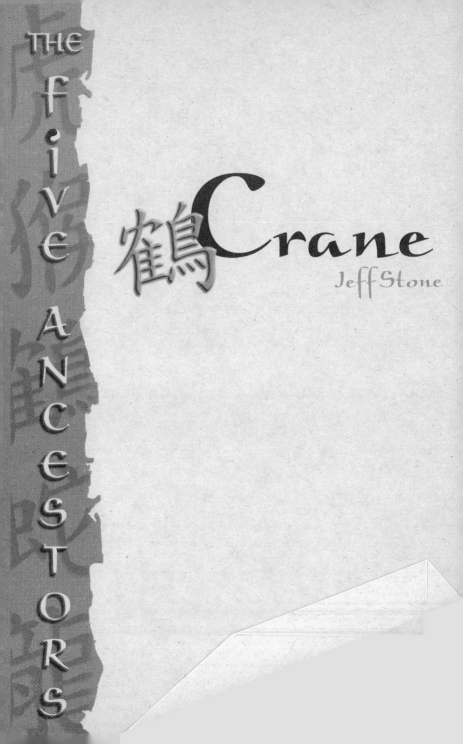

HENAN PROVINCE, CHINA

4339 – YEAR OF THE SNAKE

(1641 AD)

# PROLOGUE

"I don't understand, MaMa," said three-year-old OnYeen with a sniffle. "Why are you cutting all my hair off?"

Bing set the straight razor down on a small lacquered table, next to a pile of navigation charts. She wiped OnYeen's pale, bald head with a warm towel and brushed clumps of long brown hair from OnYeen's sleeping gown. "Everyone at the temple shaves his head," Bing said. "That's the rule."

OnYeen sniffled again. "You said shaves *his* head. I'm a girl."

"This is true," Bing replied. "However, from now on you must pretend that you are a boy. Your head must also be shaved every day."

"But why?"

"Because you have to hide. Your father and I are in danger, which means you are in danger. There are people looking for all three of us. You must pretend that you are a boy in order to better fool people, and you must never let your hair grow because of its color. You are different from everyone else. You already know this."

"I know I am different," OnYeen said. "Because of Father. But I don't care. I want to stay with him. I want to stay with both of you!"

Bing set the towel down beside a glowing oil lamp. She turned toward the cabin's single porthole and stared into the night sky. "I am sorry, but we must separate. You will go to the temple where I grew up, and I will take flight in the mountains. Your father will undock this ship of his and return to the sea."

OnYeen raised her eyes to the flickering shadows on the wood-paneled ceiling. Her mind began to race. "Why can't I shave my head and dress like a boy and stay with you? You can shave your head, too. We can be boys together."

Bing sighed. "You are far too intelligent for a child your age. You know that, don't you? You cannot come with me. I am sorry."

"Then when will you come get me?"

Bing turned away from the porthole. "We must be honest about this. It may be a long time."

"How long?" OnYeen asked. Tears began to dribble down her pale bony cheeks.

Bing knelt and looked OnYeen in the eye. "I do not know how long I will be away. Some people believe that everything happens for a reason, daughter. You must try *to find the good in this, and you must remain strong, like I've taught you. You will learn many things from Grandmaster. You will continue your training in the healing arts and kung fu. I learned everything I know at the temple."*

*OnYeen closed her eyes. "I remember Grandmaster. He came to visit once. He is mean."*

*"He is not mean," Bing said. "He is strict. There is a difference. Look at me."*

*OnYeen opened her eyes.*

*"You have to be strong," Bing said. "Going to the temple is the logical thing to do. The logical choice is always the best choice. Do you understand?"*

*OnYeen sniffled.*

*"Do you understand?" Bing repeated.*

*OnYeen wiped her eyes and nodded.*

*"Good," Bing said. "I have something for you. This has always helped me. Perhaps it will help you."*

*Bing reached into the collar of her white robe and lifted a silk thread from around her neck. Dangling from the thread was a tiny green crane. "I carved this for myself many years ago. It is jade. Some people believe the precious green stone absorbs pain. Wear it over your heart. That is where you will hurt most."*

*Bing placed the circle of thread over OnYeen's head. OnYeen didn't feel any different.*

*"I still want to come with you," OnYeen said.*

*Bing stared, unblinking, at OnYeen. She didn't reply.*

*OnYeen knew her mother was not going to change her mind. OnYeen raised her eyes to the ceiling again. "I know!" she said. "I can* dream *about you! When I get lonely, I can close my eyes and visit you. We can fly together from the mountains to the sea and find Father and—"*

*Bing shook her head and rested her long, delicate fingers on OnYeen's shoulders. "It is time for bed."*

*OnYeen frowned and climbed into her bunk. She gazed at her mother, trying not to blink.*

*"There is one more thing," Bing said. "If you think about it logically, you will understand that it must be done. We must also change your name."*

*OnYeen sank into her thin mattress and her eyelids began to quiver. "No, MaMa . . . not my name. I like my name."*

*"I like your name, too. It suits you perfectly. Perhaps too perfectly, given these troubled times. Where you are going, people speak Cantonese. They will know that OnYeen means* Peaceful, *and that it's a girl's name. I am very sorry, but we have to change it. Only Grandmaster will know that you are a girl."*

*OnYeen did her best to choke back her tears. She needed to be strong, like her mother said. She needed to do the logical thing. "What will my new name be?"*

*Bing pointed to the tiny jade crane around OnYeen's neck. "Hok."*

*OnYeen slammed her eyes shut. Tears began to leak from them again. She clinched the jade crane and wanted to cry out, but she didn't utter a peep.*

*Bing nodded approvingly. "You are a very brave girl. I am proud of you. Sweet dreams, my dearest Hok. Tomorrow we leave for Cangzhen Temple."*

# Henan Province, China
# 4348—Year of the Tiger
# (1650 AD)

# CHAPTER 1

Twelve-year-old Hok sat perched high in a tree in a dreamlike state. All around her, Cangzhen was burning. Thick black smoke rushed over her on currents of air formed by the intense heat below. Her brothers, Fu, Malao, Seh, and Long, had already taken flight. It was time for her to do the same. Grandmaster had told them to scatter into the four winds, so into the wind she would go.

Hok spread her arms wide and let the warm, rising air lift her into the night sky. She welcomed the familiar feeling and soon found herself soaring through the darkness, circling higher and higher. Yet no matter how high she flew, she couldn't escape the smoke. It burned her eyes and obscured her vision.

She had no choice but to descend once more. Maybe she could somehow fly around the trouble.

Below her, the Cangzhen compound came into view again. Through the smoky haze, Hok saw the outlines of a hundred fallen monks. She was as powerless to help them now as she had been during the attack. She frowned, and continued on.

Hok headed for Cangzhen's main gates and saw her former brother Ying just beyond them, his carved dragon face contorted into an angry scowl. Grandmaster was with Ying, and so was her brother Fu. Hok watched as Ying cut Fu's cheek with his chain whip, then blasted a large hole clear through Grandmaster's upper body with a *qiang*.

Hok shuddered and blinked, and Ying disappeared like mythical dragons were rumored to do. Fu ran away, and Grandmaster slumped to the ground.



Behind her, Hok heard her youngest brother, Malao, giggle. She glanced back, but saw no sign of him. Instead, she caught a glimpse of a monkey demon dancing across a burning rooftop—

*What is going on?* Hok wondered. She had had strange, vivid dreams before, but never one quite like this. Everything was so clear and so . . . violent.

The images got worse.

Hok saw Grandmaster suddenly stand, streams of smoke drifting in and out of the bloody hole in his chest. He glanced up at Hok soaring overhead, and his wrinkled bald head tumbled off his shoulders.

Hok shuddered again. She had had enough. She

wanted to wake up. She pinched herself—and felt it—but nothing changed. She was still gliding on smoky currents of air. She felt as if she were asleep and awake at the same time.

Perhaps the smoke had something to do with it. If she could just get away from the smoke, maybe she could find a way to wake up. Hok glided beyond the tree line, skimming the treetops. She flew as low as possible, hoping that the drifting smoke would rise above her.

She hadn't gotten very far into the forest when she passed over a large hollow tree and caught a glimpse of herself burying Grandmaster's headless body inside it. Curious, Hok landed on a nearby limb and watched herself finish the job, then drift off to sleep inside the tree.

As Hok stared through the smoky darkness, she saw a soldier with the head of a mantis sneak into the tree hollow and sprinkle something over her sleeping face.

She had been drugged. That was why she was having trouble waking up.

With this realization came a dizzying sensation. Part of Hok's mind raced back to her lessons with Grandmaster concerning certain types of mushroom spores and different plant matter that, if inhaled, could put a person into a dreamlike fog for days on end. Hok grew certain that she was now only half-asleep, which meant that she was half-awake. She made a conscious effort to pull herself into the waking world, and the smoke around her began to thin.

At the same time, Hok watched the soldier's impossible insect head in her dream. It transformed from that of a mantis into that of a man, and she recognized him. His name was Tonglong. He was Ying's number one soldier. Hok watched Tonglong lift her unconscious body and carry it out of the tree hollow.

Hok spread her arms in her dream and leaped into the air, following Tonglong. She glanced down and saw that two soldiers were now carrying her unconscious body along a trail. She was bound and hanging from a pole like a trophy animal.

Hok blinked and the scene below changed. She was now unbound, having a conversation in the forest with Fu, Malao, and a . . . tiger cub?



Hok blinked again, and a stiff breeze rose out of nowhere. It whisked the remaining smoke away, and the images went with it.

When the breeze stopped, Hok felt herself begin to tumble from the sky. She pinched herself again.

This time, she opened her eyes.

Hok found herself facedown on the muddy bank of a narrow stream. The earth was cool and moist, but the midday sun overhead warmed her bare feet and the back of her aching head. She raised her long, bony fingers to the top of her pounding temples and felt something she hadn't felt in years: hair. It was little more than stubble and caked with mud, but it was undeniable.

*How long have I been asleep?* Hok wondered. *Where am I?*

She lifted her head and her vision slowly gained focus. So did her other senses.

Hok twitched. She wasn't alone.

"You've been drugged," a voice purred from overhead. "Let me help you."

Hok looked into a nearby tree and her eyes widened. Lounging on a large limb was a lean bald man in an orange monk's robe. The man raised his bushy eyebrows and leaped to the ground with all the grace and nimbleness of a leopard. He approached Hok with smooth, confident strides.

"Dream Dust, I'm guessing," the man said. "If so, you'll be feeling the effects on and off for days. It's powerful stuff. It blurs the line between dreams and reality."

Hok stared, unblinking, at the man. If she remembered her training correctly, Dream Dust was derived from the pods of poppy flowers. Powerful stuff, indeed.

"My name is Tsung," the man offered. "It's Mandarin for *monk*. A simple name for a simple man. I am from Shaolin Temple originally, but I live outside the temple now among regular folk. Hence, my name."

Hok continued to stare.

"You don't say much, do you?" Tsung said. He stopped several paces from her, keeping a respectful distance. "That's just as well. I'll tell you what I know. I spied on your captors, Major Ying and Tonglong, for quite some time. I make a habit of keeping an eye on things in this region. I had a feeling you were something special, even before I realized you were from Cangzhen. And once I overheard them discussing the fact that you were a girl, well, let's just say that I was doubly impressed. For fighters as skilled as Ying and Tonglong to go to such lengths to bind and drug such a young captive, that's extraordinary."

Hok glanced at her wrists and ankles. They were raw and coated with dried blood, but she didn't feel a thing. The Dream Dust must be numbing the pain.

Tsung nodded at her. "Interesting outfit you're wearing. It appears large enough to fit a grown man."

Hok looked at her oversized robe and ill-fitting orange pants. She'd always worn clothes that were too large, in preparation for the days when loose clothes would better hide her gender. It seemed that didn't matter anymore. She shrugged. She didn't know what to say.

"You really *aren't* doing so well, are you?" Tsung asked.

Hok shook her head. The movement made her dizzy, and her vision began to tunnel.

"I'm taking you to Shaolin," Tsung said. "I have a horse nearby, and we will be there in no time. I'll take care of you." He flashed a toothy grin, and Hok sensed something beneath the surface. Something sinister. He took a step toward her.

Hok formed a crane-beak fist with her right hand, bunching the tips of all four fingers together and pressing them tightly against the tip of her thumb.

Tsung's smile faded. "A crane stylist?" he said. "I should have guessed."

Hok didn't offer a response.

"They say Dream Dust allows the user to see into the hearts of others," Tsung said. "Do you think this is true?"

Hok didn't respond. The world around her was growing hazy, as if smoke was drifting over her eyes. She felt her crane-beak fist loosen, her fingers relaxing into a limp open hand.

"Very interesting," Tsung purred, his feline grin returning. "Since it appears as though you're about to drift away again, I'll let you in on a little secret. My brothers at Shaolin no longer trust me, either. In fact, they haven't let me into the compound in years. However, that is all about to change. You shall be my ticket in. The ticket for me, and a few thousand of my closest friends."

# CHAPTER 2

"Open the gate!" Tsung shouted into the darkness two nights later. "A young monk needs help."

Shaolin's great front gate remained closed. No one replied.

Tsung shook his bald head and climbed off his horse, taking care to make sure Hok's unconscious body remained steadily draped across his horse's back. He untied a small pack from the horse and slung it over one shoulder. Then he slung Hok over his other shoulder and walked up the stone steps toward the gate, which was fashioned like two giant wooden doors. The doors stood higher than two men were tall, and surrounding the door frame was a gigantic brick wall, painted bright red. Set into the wall on either side of the doorway was a huge circular hole filled with intricate wooden latticework. Tsung was certain someone was peeking out through the circle on the right.

Tsung approached the huge doors and kicked them hard enough to echo on the far side. "The monk in need of care is from Cangzhen," he shouted. "A girl. You don't want her death on your shoulders, do you?"

Tsung waited for a reply. He got none. He kicked the doors again.

"Go away," a firm voice said through the latticework.

"No," Tsung replied. "Open up. I am alone. The night sky is overcast, but I am certain you can see well enough to know I speak the truth."

"We cannot afford to take any chances by letting strangers or questionable guests inside," the voice said. "Least of all you. There are soldiers about. We believe troops are gathering in the area. You might be part of it."

"Don't be ridiculous," Tsung said. "I am alone, and the girl is unconscious. Come see for yourself."

The person behind the latticework shuffled over to the great doors, and after a series of bolts were disengaged, one of the doors opened a crack.

Tsung took two steps back, and the door opened farther. An elderly monk poked his bald, wrinkled head out. He scowled at Tsung.

Tsung raised his bushy eyebrows and glanced at Hok hanging over his shoulder.

The old monk sighed and approached Tsung, reaching out to touch Hok's face. He lifted first one eyelid, then the other. "Dream Dust," he said.

Tsung nodded. "That's what I think, too. It was Major Ying's doing. He and his number one soldier, Tonglong. They destroyed Cangzhen, you know."

"So I've heard."

"This girl might have information about the attack," Tsung said. "I have information to share, too. I did some spying on Major Ying and Tonglong."

"I am more concerned about healing this child," the old monk said. "What is in this for you?"

"You know how I feel about Major Ying. If he shows up here and attempts to destroy Shaolin like he did Cangzhen, I want you to crush him. My information will help you. I'm assuming hers will, too."

The old monk ran a hand over Hok's robe. "She does appear to be from Cangzhen. Their robes are noticeably different from ours. It seems I will have to trust you. I will call a meeting immediately. Take the girl to the female guest quarters at the back of the main dormitory and meet me in the banquet hall. She will stay with us as long as she wishes, but you will not. You will leave as soon as the meeting has concluded."

Tsung nodded and shifted Hok to his other shoulder. "I will make sure the girl is comfortable before joining you. It shouldn't take long."

"You're right," the old monk replied. "It shouldn't take you long at all. People will be watching you throughout the compound. Once you step inside, you will be locked in with more than a thousand warrior monks. Do not attempt anything foolish."

Tsung waved one hand casually. "I wouldn't dream of it."

The old monk stared hard at Tsung. "Come inside, then. The sooner you are out of here, the better."

# CHAPTER 3

Hok woke with a start from a long, deep sleep. She was nauseous and her head ached. She sat up in a strange bed and rubbed her weary eyes.

She found herself in one corner of a very dark room. Only a few stray rays of moonlight crept in through old wooden shutters, but Hok swore she saw tendrils of smoke in the air. Was she dreaming again? She didn't think so. She glanced around for clues to her whereabouts and saw nothing of significance. However, as her other senses began to clear, she started to hear and even smell things that made her heart race.

Hok identified the distinct clang of wood against metal as staffs clashed with broadswords outside her room. She also recognized the rotten-egg smell of burned sulfur in the air, which went hand in hand with the *BOOMs!* that rang out continuously, usually followed by pain-filled screams. If she had to guess, she would say that soldiers were fighting warrior monks outside. She must be at Shaolin Temple, like Tsung had talked about.

Hok glanced down and was alarmed to see that she was only wearing her undergarments. She didn't recall taking off her robe. She scanned the room again, but saw no sign of her orange robe and pants.

Next to the bed was a small dresser. Hok hurried through the drawers. The only clothing inside was a red silk dress, so she stood and slipped it on, quickly pushing the knots of thread along the right side of the dress into the loop fasteners.

Hok straightened the dress's short sleeves and flipped up the high traditional collar. Her hand brushed against her collarbone, and she paused. She hurriedly ran her fingers under the collar until she caught a single silk thread, lifting it until a tiny jade crane popped free. Hok sighed and tucked the crane back into the dress.

A tremendous *BOOM!* thundered outside Hok's window, and the building shook so hard, dust drifted down from the rafters. Hok knew she was going to have to leave. She took a step on unsteady legs, and the door flew inward on its hinges.

A huge soldier filled the doorway. His armor glimmered in the light of the torch burning in his hand.

"Well, well," the soldier said. "What do we have here?"

Hok felt a burst of nervous energy jolt her system, and it cleared her head. She glanced at the dress and knew exactly what she needed to do. She looked the man in the eye and sat down on the stone floor, pulling her knees to her chest. She wrapped her arms tightly around them, shivering as though nervous.

"Don't be afraid, little lady," the soldier said with a crooked smile. "Here, give me your hand—"

The soldier stepped forward and leaned over Hok, his arm outstretched. When his fat, dirty fingers touched Hok's cheek, she latched on to his wrist with both hands. She kept her knees tucked close to her body and rolled onto her back, pulling the man toward her.



Off balance, the big man teetered forward and Hok slammed both her feet into his chest as hard as she could while still holding on to his wrist and still rolling backward.

The soldier's momentum sent him sailing in an upside-down arc over Hok's head. As soon as the man's body was beyond her, Hok let go of his wrist. The soldier continued his flip backward and crashed into the far wall. Hok hopped to her feet and sailed through the doorway.

Outside, Hok found herself facing the back of a long, low building. The night air was heavy with smoke and she couldn't see which direction would be best to run. She chose left. She reached the edge of the long building and peered around the corner.

Hok saw groups of soldiers battling individual monks. The monks were vastly outnumbered. Orange-robed bodies lay everywhere, riddled with large red holes. The monks didn't stand a chance against the *qiangs*.

Behind her, the soldier she'd sent soaring through the air cried out, "I just flushed a girl in a red dress! She is *mine*! I—"

Hok didn't wait to hear another word. She glanced left, right, and left again, trying to decide which way to run. Then she looked up. She saw a large section of roof rafter dangling from the corner of the long building. Hok squatted low and leaped silently straight into the air. Her years of crane-style leg exercises paid off. She caught hold of the rafter and swung her lightweight body onto the roof's clay tiles.

Hok stepped carefully away from the edge, up the roof's steep slope, then tiptoed across the roof tiles, moving as quickly as possible. With every step, she noticed the tiles growing warmer. There must be a fire raging beneath. She had to be extra careful now. The tiles would soon begin to fracture from the heat.

Hok was halfway along the length of the building when her luck ran out. One of the tiles beneath her feet shattered, and several pieces tumbled to the ground.

The soldier hunting Hok looked up. "My, you are a sneaky one!" he said with a laugh, and ran toward her.

Hok decided to trade silence for speed. She started to run, too. As she neared the end of the building, she realized she would either have to jump onto the next rooftop or leap down and fight the soldier. The next building was farther than Hok would have liked, but she decided she had no other choice. She spread her arms wide and soared off the edge in full stride.

Hok landed softly on her feet on the neighboring rooftop with plenty of room to spare. Below her, the soldier whistled.

"I would have never believed it if I hadn't seen it," he said. "What are you going to do for your next trick, dance? I've got something to make you dance!"

The soldier reached under his armored chest plate, and Hok began to run again. The soldier cursed and followed.

After just a few strides, Hok's heart sank. This rooftop was a dead end. There was nothing beyond it but blackness. She had to stop.

"Ready to dance for me?" the soldier asked from below, out of breath.

Hok ignored him. She glanced over the soldier's shoulder and noticed a wall just beyond his torch's glow. They must be at the far side of the compound.

In the past, Grandmaster had made her jump from the top of Cangzhen's tallest building, over its compound wall, and land on the ground beyond. She wondered exactly how high she was now, and what the dimensions of Shaolin's walls were.

The soldier reached beneath his armor again and Hok stepped farther up toward the peak of the roof. She noticed that the roof tiles were much warmer up there than they had been by the edge. In fact, they were so warm that she found she needed to shift her weight from foot to foot. That gave her an idea. Hok dropped to her knees, formed a crane-beak fist, and slammed it into one of the roof tiles.

The roof tile shattered and flames shot up through the opening, licking the night air.

"Hey!" the soldier called out, fumbling with something. "What are you doing?"

Hok stood and tore the sleeves off her dress, then tied them around a chunk of the shattered roof tile. She left the ends of silk dangling extra long and held on to one piece while lighting the others with the flames dancing up through the hole. With the flaming bundle at her side, Hok headed for the far edge of the roof, toward the compound wall.

"Where do you think you're going?" the soldier asked. "You'll kill yourself over there! Stop!"

Hok glanced back over at the soldier and saw that he was now holding a short *qiang*. She had to act fast.

Hok swung the fiery bundle over her head and hurled the flaming mass into the night. As it flew, she caught a glimpse of the compound wall and the ground beyond it. She made her best guess of the wall's dimensions and her distance to the ground beyond it.

And then she jumped.

# CHAPTER 4

Hok landed without a sound on the far side of the compound wall. She rolled several times on the damp grass to disperse the energy of her landing, and hopped to her feet.

Like Cangzhen, Shaolin had a grassy moat around its perimeter to make it harder to approach without being seen. Hok ran across it. She made it to a pitch-black tree line some distance away and stopped to catch her breath. Though smoky, the night air was much clearer here than it had been inside the burning compound. Hok inhaled deeply. Repeatedly. She was still nauseous from the Dream Dust, but this was no time for a long rest.

Hok glanced around, and froze. She realized that she wasn't alone.

Overhead, a smooth voice purred, "That was quite a leap you just made. I'm glad you announced your intentions by waving that burning projectile beforehand. Otherwise, I might have missed you entirely."

Hok looked up and saw Tsung crouched on a large tree limb. He was wearing her Cangzhen robe.

Hok's eyes narrowed.

"I told you that you were going to be my ticket into Shaolin," Tsung said with a laugh. "Borrowing your robe to wear while I did my dirty work will make for great rumors, don't you think? My men have no idea that it was me who killed Shaolin's sentries from within and opened the main gate for them. They think it was you! A Cangzhen monk other than Ying responsible for the downfall of the mighty Shaolin Temple! The people of this region will be furious! It's a shame you won't be around to witness it firsthand."

Hok's mind began to race. She wondered if what he was saying was true or just a trick to distract her.

A beam of moonlight slipped between the leaves and illuminated Tsung's shoulders. Hok saw them flex ever so slightly, and she knew what was about to happen.

Hok leaped backward as Tsung exploded out of the tree. He landed in the exact spot where she had been standing. Hok couldn't believe a human could move that fast.

Tsung grinned his toothy grin. "You're very perceptive. That's good. It will make this kill all the more exciting—"

Tsung lunged at Hok again, and Hok hopped

sideways. She escaped the brunt of the impact, but Tsung reached out at her throat as he passed by. His long fingernails connected with a glancing swipe and five thin lines of blood oozed horizontally across the side of her neck.

Hok knew that she had to take action. Tsung was far too fast for her to respond defensively, especially with the Dream Dust still in her system. As soon as Tsung hit the ground, Hok lunged at him, swinging her right elbow at his head.

Tsung's bushy eyebrows shot up in surprise and he grabbed her incoming elbow with his left hand. Hok heard him grimace as her bony elbow made contact with his palm, but he didn't release her. Instead, he tightened his grip and latched on to the back of her arm with his other hand.



Tsung began to dig his long fingernails into Hok's arm, and she responded by forming a crane beak with her free hand. She swung it at his face, expecting him to release at least one of his hands to block it. He didn't. Instead, he simply turned his head to one side and let Hok strike him. Hok nearly took out his eye. Blood began to run from the spot where she had hit him.

Hok was confused. She pulled back her free arm to strike Tsung again, and Tsung went on the offensive. Still gripping Hok's right arm with both hands, he yanked her to one side and kicked her legs out from under her.

Hok landed hard, the side of her face colliding with the ground. She felt Tsung let her arm slip through his hands until her wrist reached his fingers, and he clamped down powerfully with both hands, locking on to her wrist. With her arm now outstretched in his hands, Tsung dropped to the ground on his back, perpendicular to her, and thrust each of his legs on either side of her outstretched arm.

Hok found herself flat on her back, trapped in a straight-arm lock that she could not escape from. Tsung had a firm grip with both of his hands on her right wrist, her arm clamped tightly between his thighs. The back of Tsung's left leg was over her shoulder, and the back of his right leg was across her chest. Hok was pinned to the ground with her arm painfully outstretched.

"I bet they never taught you that move at Cangzhen," Tsung said. "Great fun, isn't it?" He laughed.

Hok's eyes began to water from the strain she felt on her arm. Tsung raised his hips slowly, and Hok felt her elbow hyperextend in a direction it wasn't designed to move—inside out.

Hok tried to pull away, or shift left or right, or do something, but it was no use. The more she pulled, the worse it hurt. She began to breathe in great gulps. Hok felt the sinews in her arms begin to pop. Her outstretched arm was going to snap. She wanted to scream, but she held it in.

"Hurts, doesn't it?" Tsung purred. "You think this is bad? Wait. After I break your arm, I'm going to dislocate every joint in your body, one at a time—"

Hok knew the end of her arm was near. She would soon lose her life, too. She had to do something.

Without another thought, she thrust her hyperextended elbow skyward and twisted her body as hard as she could to one side.

Hok heard her arm snap before she felt it, a clean break somewhere below the elbow. She cried out, but continued to twist.

Tsung's grip faltered, and Hok yanked her mangled arm free. She hopped to her feet and raced into the trees, cradling her broken arm as tears of pain cascaded over a badly bruised cheekbone. It even hurt to cry.

Hok had always had an unnatural ability to travel silently through dense forest at an amazing rate, and she used this to her advantage. She heard Tsung following her, but she could tell he was falling behind. She knew that he was incredibly fast in short bursts, but those bursts drained him of energy. He could not keep up with her over long distances.

Hok stayed on the move until her legs were wobbly and her knees swelled. And then she ran some more. Eventually, she came to a stream.

Still cradling her arm, Hok waded in above her ankles and followed the stream for several *li* through the darkness. She remained in the cold water the entire time. Her bare feet grew numb, which made walking difficult, but she stayed in the water because it meant there would be no tracks for Tsung or anyone else to follow.

As the sun began to rise, Hok saw a point where the creek forked. Unsure which branch to follow, she stopped and glanced down both routes. She needed to find a place to rest. For no particular reason, she decided to take the left branch. However, after taking a step in that direction, she detected movement out of the corner of her eye. Some distance down the right branch was a large bird wading in the water. It had a snow-white body, a black neck, black wing tips, and a brilliant red crown on its head. It was a crane.

Hok turned toward the bird, and it flew off downstream. She decided to follow it. She didn't have to walk very far before the stream suddenly opened into a wide marsh—the perfect resting place. The crane was gone.

Hok unhooked two of the loops on the side of her dress and carefully slid her broken arm into the space like a crude sling. With her one good arm, she managed to collect enough marsh grass to form a small pile on the shoreline, and she finally collapsed into the makeshift nest like an exhausted bird that had lost her flock.

# CHAPTER 5

Twenty-nine-year-old Tonglong pulled hard on his horse's reins, stopping the black beast at the wide-open gates of Shaolin Temple. It appeared he'd missed a history-making event. Shaolin was destroyed. That was good news for the Emperor.

It was even better news for Tonglong.

Tonglong adjusted his long ponytail braid over his shoulder and scanned the area. The attack must have occurred at least a day and a half earlier. He couldn't help but grin at the rows of neatly stacked corpses rotting in the midday warmth. Whoever was behind such a methodical operation had to be mad. Some of the buildings were still smoldering, but the victims had already been accounted for and the troops had moved on. It could only be Tsung, the former Shaolin monk who was now a general within the Emperor's ranks. Renegade monks like Tsung and Ying seemed to be favorites of the Emperor these days. Tonglong hoped to change that soon.

Tonglong maneuvered his horse around the far side of the compound to see what else there was to see. Halfway across the grassy expanse that separated the walls of Shaolin from the tree line, a strange object caught his eye. He climbed off his horse and picked it up. It appeared to be a strip of red silk tied around a fragment of roof tile. Most of the silk had been burned.

Puzzled, Tonglong dropped it and led his horse over to the tree line. There he found signs of a scuffle. He scoured the ground and noticed something tiny and green and glimmering.

Tonglong knelt and found a small jade crane connected to a single strand of silk. He recognized it as Hok's. Women typically hung jewelry from their sash in much the same way men hung storage pouches, but he had seen Hok wearing this around her neck.

Tonglong's eyebrows raised. He tied the string around his own neck and slipped the crane into the folds of his robe. Hok had no value to him, but Fu and Malao did. They had the dragon scrolls that Ying so desired. Tonglong desired the scrolls, too, but for a different reason. Ying wanted the scrolls to learn dragon-style kung fu. Tonglong wanted them to take over the world.

In truth, Tonglong only desired one of the dragon scrolls—the one that was rumored to contain a map to a hidden treasure vault. If the rumors were true, the vault contained enough valuables to hire an army large enough to control an entire region. And if conditions were right and things were planned properly, that army might even be large enough to take over the entire country, and who knows what else.

Tonglong knew that he was going to have to take things one step at a time, as he had been doing. When he had let Hok, Fu, and Malao escape a week ago, he had overheard them discussing Shaolin. If Hok had been here, perhaps her brothers had been here, too. Or, even better, perhaps her brothers hadn't arrived yet.

# CHAPTER 6

Hok had no idea what day it was when she finally woke to excruciating pain. Judging by her parched lips and the swelling in her face and broken arm, she guessed she'd been asleep more than one day. Probably closer to two. The extraordinary number of insect bites on her arms, legs, and head seemed to confirm as much.

Hok touched her broken right forearm and shivered. It hurt more than any injury she had ever had, and she knew the pain was going to get a lot worse before it got better—she was going to have to realign the bones. She had learned how to treat injuries like this as part of her training at Cangzhen, but she had never done it to herself. Hok stared up at clouds forming over the afternoon sun and decided to take care of it right away.

She sat up, and the marsh began to spin before her. Hok turned toward the forest's edge and saw nothing but a whirl of birch bark and willow branches. She closed her eyes, counted to one hundred, and opened them again. The world slowly came back into focus.

Hok sighed. The Dream Dust was still definitely with her. This wasn't going to be easy.

Hok laid her left hand on her broken right forearm and gently applied pressure to the swollen area with her index finger and thumb. As she felt around the break, her eyes began to water and her hands trembled.

Hok knew that a person's forearm was actually two separate bones. She determined that only one of the bones had snapped, up near her elbow. The separated pieces were misaligned, but still seemed to be touching. She knew she was lucky. She had assumed a person's elbow would have been dislocated and twisted apart attempting to escape an armlock like that. Broken bones could heal. Snapped sinews in your elbow could not.

Without giving it a second thought, Hok pinched the break with her powerful fingers. Years of crane-beak fist exercises gave her a stronger grip than most grown men. She felt the broken bone segments in her forearm grind against one another briefly, and she cried out as they shifted back into their intended position.

Hok collapsed into her marsh grass resting place. Beads of cold sweat coursed through the dirty brown stubble on her head. The sweat ran down her bruised face and mixed with her tears. Her chest began to heave. The marsh started spinning again, and Hok closed her eyes for a long time. When she finally opened them again, she knew what she needed to do next. She needed to make a plan.

When Hok thought about everything she had experienced recently, her arm suddenly seemed to be the least of her worries. She began to wonder about her brothers, Fu, Malao, Seh, and Long. Where were they? Should she go look for them? Maybe they needed her help? She also thought about all the death and destruction at Cangzhen and Shaolin, and what it might mean to the region. And then, finally, for the first time, she began to think about herself.

Growing up pretending to be something she was not—a boy—meant Hok had spent most of her time worrying about other people. How they saw her. What they thought about her. Focusing all her attention on everyone else was normal for her, but the only person she could help right now was herself. So, what was she going to do about it?

Hok felt the presence of another creature nearby, and she stared along the edge of the marsh. It was the red-crowned crane. She watched it wade slowly in her direction in search of its next meal. Hok tried to remember the last time she'd eaten. She thought she recalled having a dream in which Tsung fed her some *conjee*—rice porridge—but she wasn't sure.

The crane continued to wade in her direction, and Hok reached for the tiny jade replica around her neck. Her fingers brushed against the tall, open collar of the red silk dress, but failed to connect with the silk thread that held the crane. It was gone.

Hok ran her fingers along the five razor-thin scabs on the side of her neck, now covered with insect bites. She remembered Tsung had swiped her with his fingernails. That must have been when she lost the crane.

Fresh tears formed in Hok's eyes. Until that moment, she had never realized how important that little piece of jewelry was to her. She knew it was from her mother, but her mother was only a distant memory.

Hok decided she needed to do something to occupy her mind. Something to help herself. She stood, and the crane squawked. It stared straight at her, bobbed its head three times, and flew off.

Hok teetered in the soft soil next to her grass pile, watching the crane fly up a narrow stream not too far away. It was not the same stream she had followed to the marsh. With no other plans, Hok decided to follow the crane again. She regained her balance, took a long drink of water, and began to walk, cradling her broken arm.

Hok headed back into the forest, following the crane's path up the stream. The crane was nowhere to be seen, but Hok pressed forward. The more she walked, the more cloudy her head became. She assumed it would have gotten clearer, but she was wrong. Between the Dream Dust and stress of her arm break and everything else, she knew exhaustion was setting in. Walking was probably one of the worst things she could be doing to her body right now, especially since she hadn't eaten in a while. However, she didn't know what else to do. She didn't see any point in sitting still, waiting for help that would never arrive.

Hok continued to follow the stream, hoping it would lead to a house or a trail or something. She knew that if you followed a river or stream long enough in that region, chances were good you would eventually find civilization.

Overhead, the clouds continued to thicken and it began to rain. She was soaked and chilled to the bone in no time, but at least the rain kept the insects away and washed much of the mud off her body and out of her stubbly hair.

The evening shadows came early thanks to the rain, and Hok knew that she would have to stop soon. The dizziness was returning, too, and her mind was beginning to play tricks on her. She even thought she heard voices.

Hok rounded a bend and her thin eyebrows raised. She saw two women, one old and one a few years older than herself.

"Would you get off that bridge already?" the old woman grumbled from the stream bank. "We are going to be late."

"But I want to make a wish, Mother," the young woman replied from beneath a delicate umbrella. "Give me a coin so I can throw it into the water and—"

The young woman stopped in mid-sentence as Hok stumbled up the center of the stream, heading for the bridge.

"What on earth is that girl doing?" the old woman said in a disgusted tone. "She is far too old to be playing in the water, or in the rain for that matter."

"I don't think she's playing," the young woman said. "Look at her face and the way she's holding that one arm. She looks like she needs help."

"She needs to learn how to carry herself like a lady," the old woman snapped. "*That's* what she needs. She's a mess! There is no excuse for a girl to look like that. I bet she's homeless. Let's go before she starts begging for money."

"I don't know . . . ," the young woman said. She stepped off the bridge, and Hok tried to call out to her. All Hok could manage was a high-pitched squeak. Hok reached the bridge and collapsed onto the stream bank.

The young woman stepped forward and examined Hok, and her eyes widened. "Look, Mother! Her eyes are almost round, and the little bit of hair she has is brown!"

The old woman scoffed. "Don't touch her. She's a half-breed. No better than a mongrel dog. Come, let's be on our way." The old woman turned away from the bridge and walked up the narrow road.

The young woman looked at Hok, then at her mother. She laid her wishing coin in Hok's hand and followed her mother.

The next morning, Hok found herself still fading in and out of consciousness beside the bridge. The rain had stopped, and numerous groups of travelers had passed over the bridge since daybreak. Many had stopped to stare at her and debate how she had come to rest there, but none had offered any assistance. The only person to come near her did so just long enough to snatch the coin from her hand. She heard the word *mongrel* many times.

With her weary eyes closed to the morning light and the indifferent passersby, Hok eventually heard the strangest sound. It was a soft, garbled mumbling, like she imagined a spirit might sound.

*"Xy you zwqd vmxp?"*

Hok opened her eyes, then slammed them shut again. This couldn't be happening.

She took a deep breath and opened her eyes once more. Hok felt the remaining color drain from her pale face. She decided she must be dead. A ghost was standing over her in broad daylight.

*"Xy you need vmxp?"*

Hok blinked several times. The ghost was still there. It looked like it was waiting for her to say something. Was the ghost trying to communicate with her?

Hok stared at it. Alive, the ghost would have been a teenage boy. His face would have been pleasant enough, but now it was creamy white and covered with red dots. Its eyes were as blue as deep river water, and its hair was the color of dirty straw.

The ghost looked frustrated. It mumbled again, this time very slowly.

*"Do . . . you . . . need . . . help?"*

Hok's eyes widened. This wasn't a ghost. It was a boy! A *guai lo*. A ghost man. A white person. The boy was speaking Mandarin, but with a very thick accent. Hok could barely understand him. She nodded.

"I am going to pick you up," the boy said slowly. "Don't be afraid."

Hok nodded again.

The boy lifted Hok off the muddy stream bank and crossed the bridge. Hok noticed that he was very strong. His broad shoulders stretched his gray peasant's robe to its limits. She glanced down and saw that her dress and much of her body were streaked with mud and soaking wet, but the boy didn't seem to mind.

The boy shifted Hok in his arms, cradling her, and her broken arm pressed against something rigid beneath his robe, across his chest. It felt like a metal pipe. She winced.

"Sorry," the boy said, glancing at her arm. "Is it broken?"

"Yes," Hok whispered in a weak voice.

"Don't worry," the boy said. "I know someone who can fix you up. She's Chinese, but she won't treat you any differently. She understands people like you and me because her husband is one of us . . . fair-skinned, I mean."

Hok felt her heart begin to beat a little faster. She couldn't help but think about her father, even though she remembered almost nothing about him.

"My name is Charles," the boy said. "I come from a faraway place called Holland. I usually live on a ship, but recently I've been spending time helping my captain's wife here on land. Have you ever seen the sea?"

Hok's head began to spin. "I . . . I . . ."

Charles frowned. "I'm sorry. I shouldn't ask you to talk right now."

Hok nodded weakly.

"Try and rest," Charles said. "I'll take care of you. I promise. Pale people like us need to stick together!" He smiled.

Hok smiled back and closed her eyes. Perhaps what Tsung had said about Dream Dust was true. She seemed to be able to see into this boy's heart, and she saw he spoke the truth. Exhausted and comfortable in Charles' arms, Hok drifted off to sleep.

Images of a tall white man with a thick brown beard and green eyes filled Hok's head. It was her father. In her dream, he held one of her hands, and a tall, beautiful Chinese woman held the other. The woman had high cheekbones and tiny piercing eyes. Hok could never forget her mother's face. Hok looked up to ask her mother a question, but her dream was cut short by a high-pitched squeal and a young girl's demanding voice.

"What happened to *her*?"

Hok opened her eyes and found she was on a narrow trail, still in Charles' arms. She was also nose to nose with a fair-skinned little girl who spoke perfect Mandarin. The girl's eyes were Chinese, but her hair was long and brown.

"She looks like a drowned rat," the little girl said to Charles. "And what happened to her hair? Does she *want* to look like a boy?"

"She does not look like a boy," Charles replied.

The little girl scoffed. "Yes, she does, especially with those bruises. Where did you find her?"

"There is a bridge up the trail," Charles said. "She was lying next to it."

"You're not thinking of having her stay with us, are you?" the girl asked. "Mother is going to be sooooo angry with you."

Charles laughed. "She's not my mother."

The little girl stamped her foot. "You are going to be in so much trouble. We can't afford another mouth to feed."

"*We can't afford another mouth to feed,*" Charles mocked. "What kind of six-year-old says things like that?"

"A smart one," the little girl said. "And one that's very mature for her age." She stuck out her tongue and ran up the trail, around a bend.

Charles chuckled and looked at Hok. "That's GongJee, which means *Princess* in Cantonese. It's not her real name, but that's what she demands everyone call her. She can be a pest sometimes, but you'll get used to her. She's very smart. She can speak Mandarin and Cantonese, and she even learned Dutch from listening to me talk with her father."

Hok felt a chill trickle down her spine. The word *Dutch* sounded familiar.

"Look," Charles said, pointing down the trail.

GongJee appeared around the bend, walking next to a tall Chinese woman who was pulling a small cart. The woman wore a snow-white turban on her head, pulled low across her brow so that it obscured her features. To Hok, it made no difference. She would never forget those high cheekbones and tiny piercing eyes.

Hok watched in disbelief as her mother, Bing, let go of the cart and began to jog up the trail with long, graceful strides. GongJee tried to keep pace at Bing's side, a confused look on her face. "MaMa, what's wrong?"

Charles glanced up. "Bing? Is everything okay?"

Hok's mother glided to a stop in front of Charles. "Nothing is wrong," she whispered. "Everything is better now. Absolutely everything." She gently swept Hok out of Charles' arms, into her own.

Hok locked eyes with Bing, and suddenly felt three years old again. They held each other's gaze, and nine years passed in a single heartbeat.

"What's going on!" GongJee demanded.

Charles glanced at Bing's face, and then at Hok's. A huge smile spread across his lips. "GongJee," he said, "you know how your mother sometimes gets sad when she thinks about your 'secret' big sister? Well, I don't think she's going to be sad anymore."

# CHAPTER 7

The next several weeks were a whirlwind for Hok. She spent nearly every waking moment with Bing, and felt more like she was getting reacquainted with an old friend than reuniting with a parent. Bing didn't talk much, but Hok felt a level of comfort around her that she'd never experienced with anyone else. That made her feel good. Emotionally, at least.

Physically, things were different. Everything was taking longer to heal than Hok would have liked. Her facial bruising was still quite evident, and it took a long time for the effects of the Dream Dust to wear off. She experienced a couple of difficult nights where she lay trembling and sweating uncontrollably. At least that was now behind her.

Hok kept her broken right arm wrapped tight against her body in a silk sling that matched the white silk robe and turban Bing had given her. Her arm remained swollen for days on end, but it eventually shrank back to its normal size after regular treatments with liniments she created using herbs like willow and feverfew. Bing had these items and more in various-sized jars in the cart they traveled with. As Hok was beginning to remember, her mother was an accomplished healer, too.

Little by little, Hok began to use her injured arm again, keeping it in the sling when she wasn't carefully rehabilitating it. She found the best exercise for it was practicing her basic crane-style kung fu. Using her arms to mimic wings provided an excellent range of movements for reconditioning her elbow. She only practiced under the cover of darkness, though, so as to not draw attention to herself or the others as they traveled along the trail. As Hok had come to learn, they were a secretive bunch.

Getting specific information out of her mother was sometimes difficult, and Hok often had to ask the same question several times before getting an answer. They stayed at inns along the trail and all four of them usually shared a single room, so most of Hok's information came late at night, after Charles and GongJee had gone to sleep.

Hok had learned that her mother was still on the run after all these years. Her father was, too. Hok wasn't sure where her father was right now, but wherever it was, it was less dangerous than the region they were currently in. Charles was her father's cabin boy, and her father had asked him to spend this summer with Bing and GongJee because of the trouble brewing in this region. Bing was going to get involved firsthand, and Charles was there to help.

Hok had also discovered that the four of them were currently headed to the region's capital city of Kaifeng to attend the annual Dragon Boat Festival. During the festival, Bing was supposed to meet with some of her "contacts." Hok wasn't exactly sure what that meant, but it sounded potentially dangerous. Her mother had said that she was somewhat concerned about GongJee being with them, but she also said that she had no choice. Apparently, Bing had tried to have other people care for GongJee much like Grandmaster had taken Hok under his wing, but GongJee had always run away. If Bing ever had to do something alone for several days at a time, Charles was the only one who was able to keep GongJee from running off. Though Charles and GongJee argued often, Hok could tell that they actually enjoyed each other's company.



One night, Charles and GongJee had an entire argument in Dutch, and Hok was surprised that she understood some of the words. The word that stood out most was *Henrik,* which Hok remembered was her father's name. After Charles and GongJee had drifted off to sleep that night, Hok was eager to ask her mother questions about her father. However, Bing wasn't interested in talking. She said that she had planned something for them the following morning, and a good night's rest would be a more logical thing to do than sit up talking late into the night.

Hok gave up and went to bed.

The next morning, Hok woke to an empty room. It seemed Bing really did have something planned. Hok dressed quickly, tied a white turban over her brown spiky hair, and stepped outside. She found her mother, Charles, and GongJee unloading the small cart.

"What are you doing?" Hok asked.

Charles grinned. "Bing decided she wants to practice today. You're in for a real treat!"

"Practice?" Hok asked.

Bing nodded. "Yes. You are going to practice, too. Is your arm still sore?"

Hok felt her right arm through the sling. "Yes."

"How are your legs?" Bing asked.

"Fine," Hok replied. "Why?"

"Did Grandmaster ever teach you how to foot-juggle?" Bing asked.

"Yes," Hok said. "It was part of my balance training. What is going on?"

"Let's see how well you've learned," Bing said. "Lie down on your back."

"What?" Hok said. "Here? Now?"

Bing nodded.

GongJee giggled, and Bing looked at the little girl. "Go inside and see if the innkeeper will let you borrow a stool."

GongJee clapped her hands excitedly and ran inside.

Hok had no idea what was going on. She stared at Bing.

Bing stared back, unblinking. "Well?" Bing said. "Are you going to lie down or not?"

Hok looked at Charles, and Charles nodded back approvingly. Hok adjusted her turban and lay down on her back at the edge of the dirt trail.

GongJee came running out of the inn with a wooden stool in her arms and handed it to Bing. The three-legged stool was about knee-height, and Hok expected Bing to set it down and stand on it in order to reach something inside the cart. Instead, Bing hurled the stool at Hok.

Hok instinctively raised her legs and caught the stool with the soles of her feet. Bing had thrown it seat-first, providing Hok with a wide, flat platform. Hok bent her legs to absorb the impact, and she rotated her hips up and pressed her legs skyward, sending the chair spinning into the air.

From that point forward, everything was second nature to Hok. She had nearly forgotten about stool juggling. It was something she'd first learned when she was GongJee's age. More recently, she'd juggled much heavier items like blocks of stone to increase her leg strength as well as to improve her balance.

"Hey, you're good!" Charles said as Hok spun the stool end over end with her feet.

"Grandmaster taught you well," Bing said. "Can you juggle any other common objects?"

"Yes," Hok said. "Besides stone weights, I've

practiced with balls, small tables, chairs, paper umbrellas—"

"Paper umbrellas!" GongJee said. "Those are difficult!"

Charles laughed. "Yeah, GongJee always breaks them. She's not the most delicate person, if you haven't noticed."

"Hmpf!" GongJee said. "I'd like to see you do better."

"Me?" Charles said. "Foot juggling is for girls. Watch this!"

Hok stopped spinning the stool and caught it with her free hand. She sat up and watched Charles bend over into a perfect handstand. He started walking around on his hands, never faltering. "Let's see you do this, GongJee!" Charles said.

GongJee pouted.

Hok looked at GongJee, then glanced at her arm in the sling. "Hey, GongJee. Once my arm heals, I can teach you how to do that. It's not as difficult as it looks." She winked, and GongJee smiled back.

"That's enough for now, Charles," Bing said. "Come over here and give me a hand with the jars."

"Sure," Charles replied. He lowered his feet and stood up, walking back over to Bing. "Are you going to do your standard routine with the acrobats?"

Bing nodded.

"Acrobats?" Hok said.

"I planned to tell you after we'd practiced today," Bing said. "Sometimes I perform juggling tricks to earn money, especially during festivals. Charles and GongJee perform tricks, too. GongJee is already an accomplished foot juggler and Charles—well, you will have to wait until the Dragon Boat Festival begins to see his main skill."

"What is *your* specialty?" Hok asked her mother.

"Watch," Bing replied. She nodded to Charles and said, "The big one."

Charles helped Bing pick up the largest jar in the cart. They turned it over, and various-sized packets of dried herbs and other medicines spilled into the cart. Charles let go of the wide-mouthed terra-cotta jar and took several steps back. Bing held the empty jar herself. It was so big, she could barely get her arms around it.

Bing tossed the heavy container into the air and positioned her body directly beneath it. Hok's eyes widened. She was certain the huge jar would crush her mother's head as it tumbled back to earth. At the last possible instant, though, Bing flattened her back and caught the jar between her shoulder blades.

Hok watched in awe as her mother executed a series of moves that seemed to defy gravity. Bing balanced the enormous jar on everything from her elbow to her chin to the top of her turbaned head—without ever touching it with her hands. She passed it from balance point to balance point by jerking her body powerfully in one direction or another, then gracefully catching and balancing the huge jar for whatever length of time she desired. Bing was in complete control. Hok had never seen anything like it.

Bing eventually put the jar down and nodded to Hok. Beads of sweat ran down Bing's forehead.

"I've never seen anything like that," Hok replied. "Where did you learn to do it?"

"I taught myself," Bing said. "If you teach GongJee how to walk on her hands, I will teach you how to do this. What do you say?"

Hok's eyes lit up. "I would like that."

Bing nodded, and for the first time Hok thought she saw a hint of a smile on her mother's face. "Excellent," Bing said. "Perhaps we can start your training in Kaifeng. For now, we should pack up and get moving. We need to pick up our traveling pace if we plan to make it there in time for the annual Dragon Boat Festival."

# CHAPTER 8

Hok, Charles, Bing, and GongJee arrived in Kaifeng just before dark on the eve of the Dragon Boat Festival. As they passed through the walled city's enormous wooden gates, Hok was immediately struck by the onslaught of new sights, sounds, and smells, not to mention the hordes of people. Most surprising of all to Hok were the horrible conditions in which most of the people lived. Raw sewage trickled through open sewers in the streets and most of the buildings they passed were in disrepair. Many of the crowd members appeared to be homeless drifters who owned nothing more than the clothes on their backs, and a shocking number of them had lesions and other open sores on their skin.

If Kaifeng was the region's capital, why did so many people have to live like this? Hok made a point to remember to ask her mother.

They found the acrobats in a makeshift camp on the southern bank of the Yellow River, near the main bridge that connected the northern and southern banks. The acrobats lived in a collection of four large tents that they had set up on a relatively clean stretch of riverbank well away from the open sewers that emptied into the river farther downstream. Hok was relieved.

There were four acrobats, all brothers. Their names were Ming, Ling, Ping, and Ching, but no one bothered to point out which was which to Hok. Hok soon learned it didn't matter. In keeping with Bing's desire to conduct business in relative secrecy, no one ever mentioned anyone else's name while in camp.

The brothers let Hok, Bing, GongJee, and Charles have one of the tents, and after unloading a few things from the small cart, Bing announced that she was going to have a meeting with the brothers. GongJee said she was tired and wanted to go to bed, so Charles and Hok decided to take a short walk.

Darkness had settled in, and there weren't many people left along the riverbank. Hok and Charles headed for the bridge in the bright moonlight. At the foot of the bridge was a large display board that contained numerous announcements of events over the next several days. In the upper right corner of the board was a very official-looking document that made Hok's blood run cold.

"Hey!" Charles said, pointing to the document. "Is that—"

"Shhh," Hok said as she stared at a sketch at the top of the posting. "Yes, that drawing is me. Keep your voice down."

"Why?" Charles said. "Does it say something bad? I can't read Chinese."

"Just a moment," Hok whispered as she scanned the document. She couldn't believe it. Tsung hadn't been exaggerating back at Shaolin Temple.

"It's a wanted poster," Hok continued. "It says I'm an Enemy of the State because of some things that happened at Shaolin Temple. It also claims that I had a role in the destruction of my own temple, Cangzhen, considered to have been a closely guarded secret ally of the Emperor. At the bottom it also lists rewards for information on the capture of my brothers, Fu, Malao, Seh, and Long. It claims they were involved in Cangzhen's destruction, too. This is crazy."

Hok adjusted the turban on her head, glad that she'd decided to wear it until her hair grew to a respectable length. Another thing mentioned in the document was the fact that she had brown hair. Tsung must have reported that.

"What should we do?" Charles asked.

"I don't know," Hok said. "I—" She stopped in mid-sentence as her eyes passed over a second posting that also contained a sketch.

"Whoa," Charles said, pointing to the second posting. "Look at *that* guy. I wonder what happened to his face."

"That's my former brother, Ying," Hok replied in a low voice. "He thinks he's a dragon. It's also a wanted poster." She pointed to a smaller document pinned to the board next to it. "This one here is an update. It says that Ying has been captured and was thrown into prison under orders from the Emperor."

"What do you make of that?" Charles asked.

"I don't know," Hok said. "We should get back to camp."

"Yeah," Charles replied. He reached up and ripped down Hok's wanted poster.

"What are you doing?" Hok whispered. "Someone will notice that it's missing."

"Do you want me to put it back?"

Hok thought for a moment. "No, maybe it's better if we keep it."

"That's what I was thinking," Charles said. "Come on, let's hurry."

Hok and Charles returned to camp to find Bing still in her meeting and GongJee fast asleep. Hok lit a small oil lamp and sat beside Charles inside their tent. Charles removed the posting from the folds of his robe.

"Well?" he said.

"I don't know," Hok said. "What do you think?"

"I think we need to talk to Bing," Charles said. "Unfortunately, I've known her meetings to last all night. It's probably not worth waiting up for her. I think we should get some rest and talk to her first thing in the morning."

"That sounds logical," Hok said. She scratched her head and began to unwrap the turban. "It's not like anyone is going to see me if I'm in here, right? We shouldn't be in any danger."

"Right," Charles said with a yawn. He set the poster down next to Hok and stood. "I'm going to sleep. We'll talk more in the morning, okay?"

"Yes," Hok replied.

"Good night, Hok."

Hok nodded and slipped the wanted poster into the folds of her own robe. Her mind raced as she blew out the oil lamp.

"Good night, Charles."

# CHAPTER 9

Across the river from the acrobats' camp, Tonglong was busy making Dragon Boat Festival preparations of his own. Some of the troops he'd taken from Ying were now with him in Kaifeng, and he had already put them to work. The leader of the current project, though, wasn't a soldier. He was a former bandit. A very troublesome bandit.

Tonglong pointed to a large wooden dragon head lying on the riverbank. The brightly painted grooves of its ornately carved face were filled with mud. "I want that thing cleaned after you attach it to the boat," he said to the project leader. "Make sure you clean the tail, too. I don't want to be disqualified for a dirty, disrespectful craft."

"I know, I know," the enormous lump of man replied. "I'm familiar with the protocol. I was the boat keeper at the bandit stronghold for the past ten years, you know. We had dragon boats, too, and—"

"Don't talk back!" a silky voice interrupted. "Sssave your energy for tomorrow. You will need it."

Tonglong glanced into a nearby moon shadow and saw a familiar woman sitting on the ground, her legs coiled beneath her. He had no idea how long she had been sitting there. "Hello, Mother," he said.

"Greetings, ssson," she replied.

The project leader, HaMo, turned toward the woman. "You have to stop sneaking up on people like that, AnGangseh."

AnGangseh smirked and leaned into the moonlight. Her long, luxurious hair shimmered like the scales of a freshly hatched snake. "Toads are naturally sssuspicious of cobras. You'll get used to my ways."

"No, I won't," HaMo replied, turning back to the dragon boat. "I plan to take my money and get as far away from you as possible. How long before we get the treasure?"

"Soon," Tonglong answered. "Very soon." He flipped his long, thick ponytail braid over his shoulder. "What did you discover, Mother?"

"Bing has arrived at the acrobats' camp," AnGangseh said. "There were others with her, including an older girl I witnessed ssstealing a wanted poster from the foot of the bridge."

Tonglong tugged on the tiny jade crane around his

neck and grinned. "That is a wonderful discovery, indeed. Did you happen to see any of the bandits?"

"No," AnGangseh replied.

"I'm sure Mong and his gang will be in Kaifeng for the festival," HaMo said. He looked at Tonglong. "What about your little brother?"

"Half brother," Tonglong corrected. "Back at the bandit stronghold lake, I overheard Seh tell his temple brothers Fu and Malao that they were to meet Mong here in Kaifeng on the first day of the Dragon Boat Festival. From what I've seen firsthand, I have no doubt those three boys will make it here successfully. They are a determined and highly skilled bunch. Make sure you don't underestimate them."

"I won't," HaMo said. "Assuming they make it here and the bandits do, too, do you still think they are all going to get together? That seems highly unlikely to me."

"They will gather in one location," AnGangseh said. "I am sure of it. I sssuggest we continue to monitor the acrobats. Bing is with them now, and they have visited the bandit ssstronghold in the past."

"I agree," Tonglong said. "I predict the acrobats will put on a performance near the bridge. It's the most logical location because they will draw people from both shores. The bandits will attend in hopes of catching up with Bing, and the boys will follow the bandits. They will feel safe blending in with the crowd, and the crowd is where their focus will be. We should be able to attack from the dragon boats. They will never see it coming."

"Which boy has the map scroll?" HaMo asked. "Your brother?"

"*Half* brother," Tonglong corrected again. "Not that it matters one bit." He looked at AnGangseh. "Forgive me for saying this, but my connection with Seh means nothing. I will sever it just as readily as I will sever the head of anyone who gets in my way."

AnGangseh nodded once and a smirk slithered up the side of her face. "I didn't raise you to sssee things any other way. You're not like Ssseh, who ssseems to have inherited his father's sssensibilities. *Your* father would be proud."

Tonglong nodded back.

HaMo glanced sideways at Tonglong, and Tonglong scowled. "What are you looking at? Get back to work! That's what I'm paying you for, isn't it? Finish assembling the decorations on this dragon boat, then prepare the remaining craft. Tomorrow my journey to the throne picks up where my father's left off!"

# CHAPTER 10

The next morning, Hok woke early and tiptoed out of the tent while Charles and GongJee slept. She found her mother alone, stoking the campfire.

"Good morning," Bing said.

"Good morning," Hok replied. "I think."

"Is something wrong?" Bing asked.

Hok nodded and pulled the wanted poster from the folds of her robe. She handed it to her mother.

"Hmmm . . . ," Bing said as she read the document. "I should have guessed something like this would happen. Try not to let it bother you. My picture has been on that same board many times."

Hok frowned. "Oh."

"I wouldn't worry too much about it," Bing said.

"As long as you wear your turban, you will not stand out during the festivities today. There will be thousands upon thousands of people. No one will notice you."

"Are you sure?" Hok said. "I wouldn't want to get you or anyone else in trouble."

"There won't be any trouble," Bing said. "I have a white veil you can wear if it will make you feel better. It will even help conceal those pesky bruises still lingering on your face."

"Won't the veil draw *more* attention to me?" Hok asked.

Bing shook her head. "Have you noticed the number of people walking around with open sores? A veil will actually help keep people away from you. They will be afraid to catch whatever it is you are trying to hide."



"I guess," Hok said. She thought about the conditions she'd seen when they first entered the city. "I've been wondering, why is everything so dirty and dilapidated here? This is the capital, right?"

"What did Grandmaster teach you about the politics of this region?" Bing asked.

"Politics?" Hok said. "We weren't allowed to discuss that at Cangzhen."

Bing shook her head. "That sounds like Grandmaster. What do you know about the new Emperor?"

"Nothing, really. I know that Ying was working for him when he attacked Cangzhen, so I had been assuming that the Emperor was bad. However, there is another posting by the bridge that announces that the

Emperor has imprisoned Ying for 'crimes against the state.' " She paused. "I guess I don't know what to think now."

"You cannot label most people as good or bad," Bing said. "Especially people like the current Emperor. He is an opportunist, and his agendas change as often as the wind changes direction. Do you know why we are in Kaifeng now?"

Hok shook her head. "Not exactly."

"Your father and I are part of a loose group of different organizations sometimes referred to as the Resistance. Our goal is to create lasting peace and prosperity in this region, and throughout China. Things need to change, and we're trying to make those changes happen. We're trying to change the Emperor."

"Is he responsible for the conditions here in Kaifeng?" Hok asked.

"Partially, yes," Bing said. "He has taxed the people beyond all reason, leaving most of them wondering if they'll be able to afford their next meal. However, we recognize that the current Emperor is no worse nor better than the previous Emperor, or the Emperor before that. Our primary goal is to get this Emperor's attention in order to establish an open dialogue with him. Only through logical discussions can we begin to make a difference. Do you understand?"

"I think so," Hok said. "How do you plan to get his attention?"

"The old-fashioned way," Bing replied. "With war."

Hok blinked. "War?"

"More like strategic battles. Small battles where only the Emperor's soldiers will be involved."

"Why don't the people just stand up for themselves?" Hok asked. "There are far more people than soldiers, right?"

"That will never happen. The average person doesn't know how to defend himself or herself."

"You could teach them," Hok said.

Bing shook her head. "That would be a waste of time. One of my former brothers tried it and failed miserably. I warned him it wouldn't work, and in the end it cost the life of someone close to him."

"Really?" Hok asked.

Bing nodded. "My former brother opened a school right here in Kaifeng. He taught kung fu. Most of his students were reckless young men, and instead of using their training to protect themselves, they used it for unethical purposes. I witnessed it firsthand and confronted my brother, along with his number one student. The student took offense to my accusations and challenged me to a fight. It was an unfortunate situation."

"What happened?" Hok asked.

"I killed him."

"You *what*!"

"Hush!" Bing said. "Keep your voice down. I had no choice. He was a threat."

"What was he doing that was so unethical?"

"Stealing," Bing replied. "The students had formed a band of thieves and the number one student was their leader. They were quite dangerous."

"They were bandits?" Hok asked.

"No, *thieves,*" Bing said. "Bandits take action against the powerful in order to help the weak. Thieves simply steal for themselves."

"I see," Hok said. "What ever happened to your brother?"

"He ran off after the incident. I've been looking for him ever since."

"Do you think he is a thief, too?"

"I don't know," Bing replied. "Perhaps he is, or maybe he is simply ashamed. Either way, I hope to find out someday. This was several years ago, and no one I know has seen him since. There have been rumors that he still lives in this region. People claim to see him occasionally, sitting in trees with a snow-white monkey. They refer to him as the Monkey King." Bing paused. "There is something else I should probably tell you. He is your brother Malao's father."

Hok's thin eyebrows raised.

"If you ever see your little brother again," Bing said, "tell him I am sorry it worked out this way for his father."

Hok nodded. She couldn't help but think about her own father, and wonder what kind of situation he might be in. She cleared her throat.

"Could you tell me about . . . Father?" Hok asked. "I'd like to know where he is now."

"I don't know where he is," Bing replied. "He doesn't stay in any one place very long."

Hok wasn't satisfied. She didn't know why she was feeling so bold, but she decided to press further. She took a deep breath. "If you did know where Father was, would you . . . tell me?"

"Of course," Bing replied. "Do you feel like I am withholding information from you?"

Hok shrugged.

Bing looked Hok in the eye. "I am sorry if you feel that way. It is not my nature to talk much. And for your own protection, it is best if you don't know too much about what your father and I do. However, I feel you deserve to know at least a few things about your father."

Hok felt her cheeks flush. "I would really like to see him someday."

"I am certain he will welcome you with open arms. He still owns the ship you grew up on, you know. Do you remember it?"



Hok grinned. "Yes, I remember. What is he using it for now? Or is that something you can't tell me?"

Bing glanced around and lowered her voice. "He still uses it to transport large quantities of goods. Before you were born, it was a merchant vessel moving goods between China and his homeland. Now he uses it exclusively for the Resistance. Most recently, his cargo has been *qiangs*."

Hok frowned. She wasn't expecting to hear that, although it made sense if the Resistance was going to wage war at some point. She couldn't help but think about all the death and destruction caused by *qiangs* at Cangzhen and Shaolin.

"They are terrible weapons, I know," Bing said.

"But they are essential for the future of our cause. The Emperor has used them extensively this past year, and no one can argue with the results. Explosive powder was invented in China hundreds of years ago. We have been using it since in fireworks and other forms of entertainment, but men from your father's side of the world recently figured out a way to harness the powder's power for destructive purposes. They invented *qiangs,* and brought them here. Your father is well versed with these weapons."

Hok remembered bumping her arm against a round tube hidden under Charles' robe. "Does Charles carry a *qiang*?" she asked.

Bing nodded. "Two, in fact. The only time he doesn't carry them is when he performs, because they are rather volatile. He is deadly accurate with them. I've never seen him miss."

Hok wanted to ask what it was that Bing had seen Charles shoot at, but then she thought better of it. Maybe it really was better if she didn't know too much.

Bing turned the wanted poster over in her hands and leaned forward. A tiny jade crane popped out of the folds of her robe.

Hok felt her spirits sink. She ran her hand across the side of her neck and swallowed hard.

"Are you okay?" Bing asked.

"Do you remember the present you gave me when I was a child?" Hok asked. "Before you took me to Cangzhen?"

"The little crane?" Bing said. "Of course. You remember it, too?"

Hok looked away. "Yes. I never took it off. I kept it hidden beneath my robes until . . . I lost it. It was torn loose when I fought Tsung at Shaolin Temple, but I didn't realize it until later. I'm sorry. I miss it."

"Don't be sorry," Bing said. "I am flattered and honored that you wore it all that time. I will make you another."

"You will?" Hok said. "Thank you."

Bing nodded and cleared her throat. "Well, too much talk! It is time we wake up the others. We have a lot of preparations to make before our first performance this afternoon. I've been thinking that you, GongJee, and I should not perform today. Let's let the men do their show, and we'll save ours for tomorrow. How does that sound?"

"Fine," Hok said. "But I don't even know what it is the men do."

"I'm sure you'll enjoy it," Bing said, rolling up the wanted poster. "Do you mind if I keep this? I want to show it to a few people."

"Sure," Hok said. "You mean the acrobats?"

"No. While they are part of the Resistance, their role is limited. They are information gatherers more than anything else. I plan to meet with several of my former brothers after our performance today. They are the true leaders of the Resistance. I want to show it to them in case they haven't seen it yet. I also plan to introduce you to them. Or perhaps I should say reintroduce. Some of them haven't seen you since you were one or two years old."

Hok adjusted the turban on her head. "Do you think I will remember any of them?"

"I don't know," Bing replied. "Do you happen to remember any men with names like Python, Bear, Centipede, Dog, or Mountain Tiger?"

That afternoon, Hok stood along the riverbank with her mother and GongJee. Charles and the four acrobat brothers were still inside one of the tents getting ready. Hok was anxious to see what they had planned.

Hok was about a hundred paces downstream from the camp, and both Bing and GongJee held large empty baskets. The baskets would be used to collect donations during the performance. Hok held a smaller empty basket draped over one arm—her other arm was back in the sling to help keep it safer in the crowds, which were rather unruly. One man had stepped on her foot so hard, she was limping.

Hok couldn't believe how many people were now packed along the waterfront. It seemed the population of Kaifeng had grown tenfold overnight. The sights and sounds rivaled what she'd experienced when she first stepped through the city gates.

Hok turned to the river and stared at the fifty or so dragon boats already out there. Their brightly colored heads and tails glistened with fresh paint. The air was filled with the sound of drums as teams of twenty men rowed boats in practice sessions to a steady beat provided by a man with a drum sitting at the front of each boat. The drummer and rowers on each team were dressed in festive, brightly colored robes and black silk hats. Hok had never seen so much color.

The crowd began to get restless, and Hok turned toward the camp. She heard a single large drum begin to beat an infectious rhythm. People began to cheer.

*BOOM-BOOM-BOOM, BOOM!*

*BOOM-BOOM-BOOM, BOOM!*

*BOOM-BOOM-BOOM, BOOM!*

The crowd started to slowly part, and Hok saw one of the acrobat brothers approaching from their camp, pounding a very large drum with a short, thick stick. Behind him was another brother dressed in elaborate robes, wearing a gigantic mask that covered his entire head. The brother in the mask was swinging a long, stylized whip made of ribbon.

Bringing up the rear were two of the most elaborate creatures Hok had ever seen. They were four-legged and very large, with long orange hair covering their legs and bodies as well as their huge colorful heads. They looked like oversized lions.

Hok grinned. Charles' skill was lion dancing! The first lion was noticeably smaller than the other and was decorated as a lion cub. Hok assumed Charles was inside it by himself. His arms were serving as the front two legs, which would help explain why Charles was skilled at handstands.

The second, adult lion was composed of two people—one standing up who served as the front legs and controlled the head, and the other person bent over acting as the spine and back end of the animal. Hok realized that the brother with the huge mask and whip was supposed to be a lion tamer.

The excited crowd began to form a large circle, and the lions trotted into the center. People flowed in their direction in droves. Hok felt her pulse quicken as the energy level around her rose to a fever pitch. The drummer began to beat harder and louder, and the lions started to shimmer and shake. The larger lion had enormous, expressive eyes that blinked and a huge mouth that opened and closed. Even the ears wiggled.

Without warning, the lion cub leaped straight into the air onto the back of the larger lion and began to spin around and around in fast, tight circles. The crowd roared with approval. The cub leaped to the ground and rolled sideways, then popped to its four feet and began to shimmer and shake again, bobbing its head up and down. The crowd roared again.

"Here," GongJee said, and Hok felt something poke her in the side. It was a large empty basket. Bing had disappeared.

"Take MaMa's basket," GongJee said. "She'll be right back." She pointed to one end of the circle. "You walk that way, and I'll go the other way. If you fill up the basket, take it to MaMa right away. She'll give you another one. If you don't see her, the best way to find her is to whistle like a crane. Do you know how to do that?"

Hok nodded, and the veil over her face fluttered.

GongJee hurried off and began collecting coins from the crowd. Hok watched her for a moment, noticing how GongJee offered a huge smile to everyone she approached and followed each donation with a quick bow. She had obviously done this before.

Hok began to walk slowly in the opposite direction, keeping one eye on Charles' fantastic dancing and the other on the crowd. Charles really was good.

Hok had no sooner received her first coin when she sensed someone staring at her. She glanced up and nearly tripped over her own feet.

"HOK!" a squeaky little voice shrieked. It was Malao. Even more surprising, Seh and Fu were with him. All three were wearing tattered gray peasant's robes and looked different because they all had hair. Seh's was particularly thick and unruly.



Hok was glad she was wearing the veil. It hid her enormous smile. Still, she felt she had to turn away to help hide her excitement. She took a few steps.

"Hey!" Malao called out. "Why did Hok—*mmmpf!*"

Hok didn't have to look back to know what had just happened. Seh had wrapped a snake-head fist around Malao's mouth. Seh was obviously trying to not draw any attention to her, or them. Seh had always been good about things like that. Hok thought it was best to do the same. As casually as possible, she began to limp toward the camp, certain her brothers would follow.

# CHAPTER 11

"There they are," Tonglong said, pointing from the rear of his elaborate dragon boat.

"Yesss," AnGangseh replied from the bow. "I sssee."

HaMo shifted in his seat behind AnGangseh at the front of the boat. "What should we do?"

"Wait for my command," Tonglong said. He adjusted the large black hat on his head and stood, causing the long, narrow boat to wobble in the water. He cleared his throat, and twenty soldiers—ten to a side—turned to look at him.

Tonglong pointed to a circle of people on the southern shore, near the main bridge. "Our targets are there. Remember, while most of them are young, they are far from children when it comes to fighting. Their skills are superior to yours, so be sure to keep your distance. Rely on your weapons. The young monks appear to be separating themselves from the masses and heading for the camp. That is where we shall go ashore. It is time."

The men put their paddles back into the water and Tonglong glanced over his shoulder. He waved one arm, signaling to five additional dragon boats trailing close behind.

Tonglong pointed toward the camp and sat down. All six boats heaved forward collectively. The five trailing boats soon passed Tonglong's vessel and ran themselves aground about two hundred paces from the camp. One hundred soldiers disguised in festive costumes quickly stepped out of the dragon boats onto the shore and formed ranks, while Tonglong and his twenty boatmen, plus AnGangseh and HaMo, stopped their dragon boat short of the riverbank, remaining afloat.



AnGangseh pulled a large black hood over her head and slithered off her seat, sinking down to the floor at the very front of the boat. HaMo sat up straight and stared at the crowd, puffing out his sizable chest.

People on shore and on the bridge began to notice something was wrong. It wasn't normal for dragon boat teams to go ashore in a single group like that and line up like soldiers, and it was unheard of for them to be armed with spears and broadswords. The crowd began to panic. They pointed first to the soldiers, then to Tonglong's dragon boat.

Tonglong looked over at the camp and saw his half brother, Seh, standing near a fire pit, next to the young Cangzhen monks Malao and Fu. Also standing there were a woman and a teenage girl, both wearing turbans; a very young girl with long brown hair; and a white teenage boy. It was an odd-looking bunch, so engrossed in each other that they failed to see what was happening around them. Tonglong decided to give them a sporting chance. He stood, removing his hat. His long, thick ponytail braid spilled out and he adjusted it over his front shoulder.

Tonglong stared at his half brother, Seh, and shouted, "Remember me?"

Seh didn't respond. However, Fu, the aggressive boy tiger, shouted, "Tonglong!"

Tonglong smirked. "Very good, Pussycat. Now it's the serpent's turn to talk. You have something that I want. Give it to me, and we'll be on our way. Deny me, and—"

Tonglong snapped his fingers and each soldier in his boat raised a *qiang*.

The crowd lost control. Hundreds of bystanders scattered, stumbling and tripping over one another. A panic-induced tension filled the atmosphere, and Tonglong breathed it in deeply, savoring it.

Tonglong saw Seh turn away from the shore, and he followed Seh's gaze. A group of five adults was pushing toward the camp. Tonglong recognized all of them from the bandit stronghold.

In the lead was Mong, the enormous, bald, pale mountain of muscle who was AnGangseh's second husband and Seh's father. Mong meant *Python* in Cantonese. He was the bandit leader.

Behind Mong was the gigantic, hairy bandit called Hung, or *Bear,* carrying a huge pair of golden melon hammers. The group also included the iron-body kung fu bandit with dirty, stubby limbs whose name was NgGung, or *Centipede;* the crazy, big-nosed, floppy-eared bandit called Gao, or *Dog;* and a beefy man with a scraggly beard and long, matted hair that Tonglong recognized as a famous drifter often called The Drunkard, but whose real name was rumored to be Sanfu, or *Mountain Tiger.*

They were a formidable force, to be sure, but Tonglong had a hundred armed men on shore and twenty loaded *qiangs* in his boat. Tonglong knew he had the upper hand.



"Don't give up that scroll!" Mong shouted to Seh over the cries of the fleeing crowd.

Seh turned back to the river and looked at Tonglong. "I didn't plan to," he shouted.

*You had your chance, little brother,* Tonglong thought. *Goodbye.* He tucked his long ponytail braid into his sash and raised one arm high, then let it drop.

"FIRE!"

# CHAPTER 12

Shots rang out overhead as Hok retreated from the waterfront hand in hand with GongJee. Their mother was beside them, as were Charles, Fu, and Seh. Unfortunately, Malao was not with them.

As they rushed into Kaifeng's narrow streets, away from the soldiers' *qiangs,* Hok glanced at the five men with strange but familiar animal names surrounding them. These men had risked their lives to help keep Tonglong's soldiers at bay. *Bear* had been shot in the arm, and another *qiang* ball had grazed *Mountain Tiger*'s cheek. Both men were bleeding heavily, but they remained in a protective circle around Hok and the others, even now. These men were warriors, and they had very likely just saved her life, as well as the lives of GongJee and Charles, not to mention her brothers.

Warning bells rang out from the city's central bell tower, and people everywhere began to scramble to lock themselves inside their homes and storefronts. Hok was grateful because it meant they could put even more distance between themselves and the soldiers on their trail.

In order to run better, Hok had abandoned her sling and turban back at the waterfront, and Charles had stripped himself of his costume. However, Charles was grumbling about having been caught without his *qiangs*. They were still back at the camp.

Hok felt that none of them were in a position to grumble. She was just thankful to be alive. She hoped Malao was as lucky.



It seemed Fu couldn't stop thinking about Malao, either.

"We have to help Malao!" Fu complained. "Didn't you see what happened to him? We need to go back!"

"We saw what happened to your little brother," Bing said to Fu. "AnGangseh, Tonglong, and HaMo captured him. We'll discuss this at the safe house. We're almost there."

The group soon slowed down and Mong stopped in front of a small shop. There was no sign on the building. The only thing that set it apart from the other buildings on the street was a small metal phoenix in the center of the door, painted green.

Mong banged on the door three times. A moment

later, the phoenix rotated up and Hok saw a concerned eye quickly scan their group.

"Come in, come in!" a woman said in a hurried, muffled voice from the other side of the door.

Hok heard several locks disengage, and the door swung open. The group rushed inside without a word. As the woman relocked the door, Hok glanced around.

The dark, dusty room was a ramshackle dining hall. Ten small tables were randomly positioned around the space, paired with broken, mismatched chairs. The place was a mess.

"I am so glad you all made it back here in one piece, and that you've brought friends," the woman said as she straightened up. "The war bells are ringing and . . . oh, sorry. Where are my manners? My name is Yuen. Welcome to the Jade Phoenix." She bowed to Hok.

Hok bowed back.

"We don't have time for formalities," Mong said. "I am sorry. May we take shelter here? I must warn you, though, there is a chance we are being followed. Hung and Sanfu may have left a bit of a blood trail."

Yuen glanced quickly at Sanfu clutching his face and Hung gripping one arm. "Oh, dear!" she said. "Let's get you upstairs. All of you. The room above the kitchen is the safest place. It will be cramped, but you can come down after nightfall. I'll see what I can do about the blood trail once you're safely hidden."

"Thank you," Mong said. He headed for a tattered

curtain at the back of the room, and the group followed.

Hok found herself pushed into a small kitchen with the others. Yuen pointed to the far corner, and Hok saw a rope ladder leading up into a hole in the wood-paneled ceiling. "Up you go," Yuen said.

Hok watched Bing climb the rope ladder first with GongJee, followed by Charles. Fu and Seh went next. As each one grabbed the sections of rope, Hok couldn't help but think of Malao tied up somewhere.

Mong was standing next to Hok. She tapped him on the arm.

"Excuse me," Hok said. "Shouldn't we do something about our brother Malao as soon as possible? I mean, wouldn't our chances of helping him be better if we acted quickly?"

"Perhaps," Mong said. "But we must put the safety of the group first. We will develop a plan to help Malao as soon as possible. In the meantime, I don't think you should worry too much. I saw what happened, and I suspect the kidnappers intend to trade him for something Seh carries. The woman who knocked Malao unconscious—AnGangseh—could have easily killed him. Believe me, they will contact us."

"But how are they going to contact us if we are hiding?" Hok asked. "Maybe a few of us should try and rescue him. I'll volunteer."

Mong folded his enormous arms. "Tonglong will figure out a way to get a message to us. As for a rescue attempt, we have no way of knowing where they are taking Malao. Tonglong has no relationships with anyone outside of his own circle that we can exploit."

NgGung cleared his throat. "Um, Boss? What about Ying?"

"What about him?" Mong asked. "He's in prison."

"That's right," NgGung said. "The prison is only a few streets due east of here. Perhaps we could go see him and find out if he has any idea where Tonglong might have taken Malao. We'd have to make it worth his while, of course. Maybe we could offer him something?"

"From what I know about Ying," Mong said, "the only thing he would accept in exchange for helping anybody is his freedom, or possibly Tonglong's head. Unless you are prepared to offer him one of those, I doubt he'd comply."

"Can't we try?" Hok asked. She looked at NgGung. "Do you think I could sneak in there?"

NgGung stroked his long, thin mustache. "You'd have to break in, and the prison is heavily fortified with the Emperor's personal guard. Hmmm . . . If you were going to attempt it, tonight would be the night to do it. The Emperor is scheduled to lead the dragon boat festivities this evening, and he is sure to bring most of his protectors with him after this incident at the riverfront. Plus, there will be fireworks, which are always a great distraction. I've never seen a guard who didn't leave his post to watch fireworks."

"No one is breaking in anywhere," Mong said.

"The risk is not worth the payoff, assuming there would even be a payoff. We will wait for word from Tonglong about Malao. That is all. Everyone, upstairs. We need to disappear."

NgGung looked at Hok and shrugged. "I tried."

Hok nodded her thanks.

The men began to climb the rope ladder, and Hok shifted from foot to foot. She still couldn't see herself hiding at a time like this.

Yuen looked at her. "Are you okay? You seem anxious."

"I'm fine," Hok replied. "I just don't want to climb up there just yet."

"I understand," Yuen said. "I don't like tight spaces, either. If you don't mind hiding alone, I can show you a different place."



Hok thought about it a moment. "Yes, that would be nice. Thank you."

Mong was on his way up the rope ladder, and he turned to Hok. "I'll let your mother know where you're going. We'll see you in a few hours."

"Thanks," Hok replied.

"Come with me," Yuen said. She slipped through the tattered curtain, back into the main dining area, and Hok followed. They were halfway across the dining room when someone began to pound vigorously on the front door.

"IN THE NAME OF THE EMPEROR, OPEN UP!"

Hok's eyes widened and Yuen scowled. "Soldiers!"

Yuen whispered. "Upstairs, quickly! There is no time to hide anywhere else. I'll get rid of them."

Hok raced back through the curtain into the kitchen—and froze. The rope ladder was being pulled up into the ceiling. She was about to call out softly when she spotted something out of the corner of her eye. It was a small open window.

Hok glanced at the rope ladder rising higher and higher, and she thought of Malao again. If she was going to try to do something to help him, this might be her only chance.

Hok ran to the window and hopped onto the sill. She saw an empty alley outside with an easy jump to the ground. She looked back over her shoulder as a wooden panel in the ceiling began to swing closed. Beyond the tattered curtain, Hok heard the front door open.

Hok took a deep breath and sailed out the window.

# CHAPTER 13

Less than a quarter of an hour after leaving the Jade Phoenix, Hok found herself taking refuge in the overhanging roof rafters of the prison itself, waiting for the sun to go down. She was surprised how easily she'd found it. Like NgGung had said, it was just a few streets due east of the Jade Phoenix.

Fortunately for her, few people passed down the narrow street along this side of the prison, and the few who did did not look up into the eaves. As the sun began to set several hours later, however, everything changed.

Fireworks exploded in the direction of the river, and everyone started looking up. Hok heard people begin to cheer, and the small number of residents who weren't already at the riverfront raced out of their homes and shops to catch the display. Hok even caught a glimpse of two men who looked like prison guards racing along at an angle that left Hok certain they had come from the prison's front doors along the main street.

Hok decided to make her move. She soared down from her perch and landed in a silent roll, protecting her injured arm, then hopped to her feet. She ran along the side of the prison to the front of the building and poked her head around the corner. The main street was empty. She waited for a few moments, but didn't see any guards at the entrance.

Hok decided that the most obvious route might also be the best one. She headed for the prison's main doors. They were unlocked. She glided inside and drifted silently through the lantern-lit entry, keeping her body pressed tightly against one wall. Hok felt completely alone. She wondered if Ying was even there.

Hok turned the room's first corner and choked back a startled cough. In front of her was a single large cell with iron bars for a front wall and stone everywhere else. Inside it was Ying. She barely recognized her sixteen-year-old former brother.

Ying lay in the back corner, curled into a ball. His carved face had been beaten to a bloody pulp, and his eyes were almost swollen shut. He breathed through his mouth like a sick animal, wheezing loudly every time he inhaled or exhaled. His forked tongue hung out of his mouth like a dog's, lying over his pointed teeth. Ying looked like he had lost at least one-third of his body weight, perhaps more. Hok had never seen someone in such condition. He had been beaten to the very verge of death.

Based on the sound of Ying's breathing, Hok could tell that one of his lungs had been punctured, probably by a broken rib. Every breath Ying took would be utter agony. If left untreated, he would surely die a long, slow death. Someone wanted to make him suffer.

While Ying was a horrible person, Hok didn't want to see anyone have to suffer like that.

Ying seemed to sense her presence and looked up. Even through his swollen face he managed to see her. Or perhaps he sensed her *chi.* Either way, his scabbed lips twisted into a grotesque scowl. He forced himself to wheeze two words: "Go . . . away."

Hok shook her head. She approached the cell's iron bars. "I need your help."

Ying wheezed loudly several times in rapid succession. Hok realized that he was laughing. "Look at . . . me. What could I do . . . for you? What could you possibly do . . . for me?"

Hok stared at Ying's broken body. He didn't look like he would survive long without some sort of treatment. It gave her an idea.

"Malao has been kidnapped by Tonglong," Hok said. "I'm hoping you might have some idea where they took him. In return, I will prepare healing tonics for you and sneak them in here."

Ying slowly shook his head. "No . . . ," he wheezed. "I want out. . . . Get me out . . . and I will help you. . . . You have . . . my word."

Hok blinked. Break him out of prison? While the last thing she wanted was Ying on the loose, she had a strong feeling he wouldn't be able to go very far. He would most likely get recaptured. Even if he wasn't caught, he could very well die from the strain of being on the run. If he remained here, though, he would surely die. As much as she disliked Ying, she wasn't sure she could leave him to that certainty. It seemed to Hok that breaking Ying out might be the best option.

Hok stared, unblinking, at Ying. "I agree to your terms. How do I get you out of here?"

Ying nodded behind her.

Hok spun around, and froze. A man stood between her and the prison's main entrance. In his hand was a single key. "I have an idea," the man purred. "You could use *this* to get Ying out of his nest."

It was Tsung. She should have guessed Ying wouldn't have been left alone.

Hok knew to be ready for anything. She took several steps forward, putting space between the front of Ying's cell and her back. The last thing she wanted was to be pinned against something by Tsung.

"I see you are coming to meet me in the middle of the dance floor," Tsung said. "Such a forward young lady you are. Are you sure you want to do this? You'll need two good arms to swing with me, you know." He flashed a big toothy grin.

Hok didn't reply. She lowered herself into a wide

defensive stance, her good arm held out in front of her, her bad one tucked tight to her body. She wanted him to come at her.

Tsung bowed, low and deep. "Let the dance begin." He dropped the key and sprang at Hok's neck.

Hok was ready. As soon as she saw Tsung leave the ground, she dropped flat onto her back and kicked one leg straight up into the air. Her foot sank deep into Tsung's stomach as he sailed over her.

Tsung groaned as his midsection molded itself around Hok's heel. Hok used Tsung's forward momentum to help slam her leg to the ground, and Tsung went with it. He hit the stone floor with a solid *THUD!*

Tsung cursed and Hok tried to pull her leg away, but Tsung was too quick. He grabbed her foot and tucked it under his armpit, and in one smooth motion he locked both his hands around her heel and leaned back hard.

Intense pain shot through Hok's ankle. Tsung had her in some sort of heel lock. Tsung began to twist to one side, and Hok's misery was magnified tenfold.

Unsure of what to do, Hok rolled her body in the direction of Tsung's twist. She felt the pressure on her heel subside, but only for a moment.

Tsung righted himself, then twisted again in the same direction, more powerfully this time. Again, Hok twisted with him.

While the pressure on her heel subsided the second time, too, Hok felt the sinews in her ankle begin to weaken. If Tsung kept this up, they would snap just like the ones in her elbow nearly had.

Hok sensed Tsung winding up for a third twist when Ying managed to wheeze out loud, "Twist double-time, Hok!"

Tsung unleashed a mighty twist, wrenching his body around one hundred and eighty degrees. Out of options, Hok followed Ying's instructions. She twisted her body around three hundred and sixty degrees in the same direction as Tsung's twist.

It worked. Tsung couldn't maintain a firm grip on her spinning foot and she felt the pressure on her heel subside.

Ying wheezed out loud, "*Crane Spins the Legs!*"

Hok spun her free leg in a powerful arc and brought that heel crashing down onto Tsung's temple.

Tsung's body went limp, unconscious, and Hok jerked her foot free. She wondered where Ying had learned to counter a move like that. It certainly wasn't at Cangzhen.

Hok stood and looked at Ying.

Ying had managed to sit upright. He had his arms wrapped around his sides, his chest heaving. Hok realized he was chuckling. "Rescued by . . . an ax kick . . . from a girl . . . named *Peaceful*!" Ying wheezed. "Ha-ha-ha!"

Hok glared at him. "How do you know my given name?"

"I was . . . seven years old . . . when you came to . . . Cangzhen," Ying wheezed. "Sometimes I . . .

spied on . . . Grandmaster." He shrugged slightly and appeared to attempt a grin.

Hok frowned.

"I had . . . a different name . . . too," Ying wheezed. "Saulong . . . *Vengeful Dragon!* . . . I see . . . you are . . . no longer . . . living up to . . . your name. . . . Let's see . . . if I can . . . live up to . . . mine." He nodded toward the center of the room.

Hok turned and saw the key on the floor. She heard Ying begin to struggle to his feet.

Hok bit her lip, then scooped up the key. She hurried over to the cell door and opened it. She had to remember, she was doing this for Malao.

Ying stumbled forward and leaned on Hok's shoulder. "I'll talk . . . as we walk."

Hok put one arm around Ying's bony shoulders. He felt like a skeleton.

"We'll go . . . out the back door," Ying wheezed. He nodded toward Tsung's unconscious body. "Take me . . . to him first."

"No—" Hok began.

"Do it!" Ying hissed. "Look at . . . his sash."

Hok glanced at Tsung and saw that he wasn't wearing a sash at all. Instead, a chain whip was wrapped around his waist.

"I'll get it," Hok said. She gently leaned Ying against the wall for support and released him.

Ying spat on the ground. "I suggest you . . . kill him. . . . He will . . . seek revenge."

"No," Hok replied. "I'm not leaving you to die in

his hands, and he's not going to die, either." She retrieved the chain whip and looped it around Ying's neck. "Let's get moving so we can—"

Ying cocked his head. "Shhhh . . . ," he wheezed.

Hok listened closely. She heard voices from around the corner at the prison entrance.

"Whew! What a party!" a man said. "The Emperor sure knows how to have a good time!"

"Yes, indeed," another man replied. "Too bad we had to come back here—"

Ying nodded toward the far corner of the room and Hok noticed a door. As they headed for it, Ying whispered in a wet, wheezing voice, "Tonglong will take Malao . . . to a place we called . . . the Riverbank Safe House. It's an . . . old shack . . . an hour downriver . . . from the main Kaifeng bridge. It's on . . . the southern shore . . . near a willow . . . with twin trunks."

They reached the door and Hok tried the handle. It was locked, but she saw the key was still in the mechanism. She turned it and opened the door. The hinges shrieked.

"What was that?" one man called out.

Hok heard footsteps, and she pushed Ying through the doorway.

"Look!" one of the men cried. "Major Ying is escaping!"

"Who is that with him?" the other man said. "It's—it's the girl from the wanted poster!"

Hok slammed the door closed and engaged the lock with the key from the outside. She leaned Ying against the side of the building and hurried over to the building's front corner.

Hok peered out at the main street, trying to decide which way to go. She didn't know. Maybe Ying had an idea. She looked back at him, but he had disappeared, like dragons were rumored to do.

The two prison guards came barging out of the front entrance, yelling, "SOUND THE ALARMS! THERE'S BEEN A PRISON BREAK!"

Hok turned and ran.

# CHAPTER 14

"You didn't kill him, did you?" HaMo asked.

"No," AnGangseh replied. "He is only sssleeping."

"Are you sure?" HaMo said. "He hasn't moved in hours."

"I am sure," AnGangseh said. She stepped over Malao's unconscious body and handed a small bottle to HaMo. "This is what put the boy in his current ssstate. It's called Dream Dust, and it is very powerful. I make it myself. Never put the bottle near your face."

HaMo cringed and held the bottle at arm's length. "What do you want me to do with it?"

"If the boy monkey begins to wake up," AnGangseh said, "sssprinkle a tiny amount of the powder on his upper lip, beneath his nose. A sssingle dose now would keep him asleep until late afternoon."

"But the sun hasn't even risen yet," HaMo said.

"As I sssaid, it is very powerful. That bottle will last you a very long time. Keep the boy drugged, and he won't give you any trouble. Let the effects wear off ssslightly each day, though, ssso that you can feed him and give him sssomething to drink."

HaMo nodded, holding up the small bottle. "Thanks."

The front door of the safe house swung open and Tonglong stepped inside the single-room shack. He set an oil lamp on a small dusty table.

"It appears as though we are alone," Tonglong said, "though it is difficult to see. Clouds have formed over the moon."

"I sssense rain," AnGangseh said.

"Rain is fine," HaMo said. "It shouldn't affect our plan."

"I agree," Tonglong said.

HaMo scratched one of his enormous chins. "What is it we're after again? A scroll?"

"Yes," Tonglong said. "A dragon scroll from Cangzhen Temple."

"Neither of you study dragon-style kung fu," HaMo said. "What are you going to do with it?"

Tonglong looked at AnGangseh, and AnGangseh nodded.

"It's a map," Tonglong said.

HaMo burst into laughter. "A dragon scroll map from Cangzhen! You believe that old wives' tale?"

Tonglong stared at HaMo, and HaMo stopped laughing. "You're serious, aren't you?" HaMo asked.

"Deadly ssserious," AnGangseh said.

"We have reason to believe the story is valid," Tonglong said.

"The story claims there is a secret treasure horde," HaMo said. "That's a little too far-fetched for me. Besides, there was no such scroll when I lived at Cangzhen. I used to be in charge of the library. If such a scroll exists, it had to arrive at Cangzhen with the last Grandmaster, and we all know how shifty he was. You're wasting your time. Even worse, you're wasting *my* time. You promised me riches beyond belief. Well, I don't believe it. I think it's best if you just pay me for what I've done thus far, and I'll be on my way."

Tonglong straightened. "Your payment will come from the treasure. That was our agreement."

"Well, you were obviously withholding some key information," HaMo said. "I want out. What do you have that's worth something?"

AnGangseh looked at Tonglong. "If he wants out, let him out." She pointed to Malao, lying on the dirt floor. "You can have the boy, as well as the bottle of Dream Dust to keep him manageable. Take him to Jinan and sssell him to LaoShu."

HaMo scratched one of his enormous chins. "Sell him to *Rat*? That sounds appealing, but I was expecting more compensation than that. After all, I did get you access to the bandit stronghold."

"What if I were to throw in something else to

sweeten the deal?" Tonglong asked. "How much do you think LaoShu would pay for a twelve-year-old girl from Cangzhen? One who can fight."

HaMo's eyes widened. "Now that's more like it! You wouldn't be thinking of the girl dressed all in white from the acrobat camp, would you? I noticed her being protected by the bandits."

"The very same," Tonglong replied. He tugged at the silk thread around his neck and the tiny jade crane popped out of the folds of his robe.

HaMo's flabby cheeks rose up in a corpulent grin. "My friend, I think we have a deal."

# CHAPTER 15

Hok spent the night in flight, successfully steering clear of both the prison guards and Tonglong's soldiers by weaving in and out of Kaifeng's narrow streets. She stayed on the move, not daring to stop. More than anything she wished she could return to the Jade Phoenix, but the last thing she wanted to do was endanger anyone there by showing up. Besides, she wasn't sure she could find it in the dark.

Shortly before sunrise, it began to rain. Chilled to the bone and soaking wet, Hok decided to try to find shelter. She was near the river, and she began to think about the acrobat camp. The acrobats had probably fled the city, and soldiers might be occupying the camp. Still, it was worth taking a look. Even if she couldn't take shelter there, at least she might be able to find some food or dry clothes to change into once the rain stopped.

Hok was upstream from the main bridge, and she cautiously worked her way downstream along the riverbank until she neared the camp. It appeared abandoned, but in the darkness she couldn't be sure. She approached cautiously.

The first tent she came to was the one that Charles and the acrobats had used to put on their costumes before their lion dance performance. Hok remembered Charles complaining about not having his *qiangs.* Perhaps they were still inside.

Hok eased up to the back of the four-sided structure. The door flap was directly opposite her, facing the center of the camp. She would have to sneak around to the front.

As Hok silently rounded the first corner, she sensed someone nearby. She began to retreat, but she was too slow.

A boy poked his head of thick, short black hair out from under the bottom edge of the tent. He stared up at Hok in the rainy darkness.

"*Seh!*" Hok whispered.

Seh nodded and slithered from under the tent edge, over the muddy ground. He stood and pointed back upstream. He wanted to leave.

"Wait a moment," Hok whispered. "Is anyone in there?"

Seh shook his head.

"I'll be right back," Hok said. She dropped to the muddy ground and slipped into the tent. Her eyes took a moment to adjust to the darkness, but she soon saw what she was looking for—a pile of dirty clothes. Charles didn't seem like the type of person to leave his *qiangs* out in the open, and a pile of dirty clothes is exactly where Hok would hide something important.

Hok pushed the clothes aside and found a matching set of short *qiangs*. The metal barrels were scratched and discolored, and the wooden handles were well worn. These weapons had seen a lot of use. Hok wrapped them in a robe that was lying there and slipped back out of the tent.

Without a word, Seh began to run. Hok followed on his heels.

Seh led Hok much farther upstream, following the riverbank. Dawn was breaking, overcast and gray, when they finally stopped before the crooked door of a battered boathouse. Seh knocked once, paused, then knocked four times in rapid succession. The door swung open, and Hok followed Seh inside.

Mong stood just inside the doorway. He closed the door behind them and Hok glanced around. The room was dimly lit by a single oil lamp on each of the building's three rickety walls. Where the fourth wall would normally have been was nothing but open air. This wall-less section dangled out over the river, and floating on the river inside the boathouse was a small skiff. It was empty except for a long pole that

Hok knew was used to push the skiff along the shallow riverbank.

On a small section of dry riverbank inside the boathouse were Bing, Fu, and Charles, plus a girl with smooth dark skin and a curiously flat face. Hok thought the girl looked a surprising amount like an eel.

Bing smiled, and Hok walked over to Bing's side.

"I am happy to see you," Bing said.

"And I am happy to see you," Hok replied. She glanced around the room. "All of you, as a matter of fact. But where is GongJee?"

"She is with the others back at the Jade Phoenix," Bing said. "NgGung and Gao are keeping her entertained."

"Oh," Hok said. "So the soldiers did not discover you there?"

"Most of those soldiers couldn't find honey in a beehive," Mong replied. "They took a quick look around, but left soon after Yuen offered them a meal. It seems they saw the condition of her dining hall and lack of customers, and decided no one in their right mind would visit there, bandits included. If they only knew how delicious her soy sauce chicken was!" He laughed.

Hok grinned. "How about the two men who were injured rescuing us? I believe their names are Hung and Sanfu? Are they all right?"

"They are just fine," Mong said. "Those two have shrugged off injuries far worse in the past. It's considerate of you to ask about their well being, though. I'll tell them you send your regards."

"Thank you," Hok said.

Mong nodded. "So, what is it that you have in your hands? Tomorrow's laundry?"

"Oh, sorry," Hok said. She turned to Charles and handed him the bundled robe. "This is for you."

"Huh?" Charles said. He unwrapped the bundle and his face lit up. "You went back and got these for me? Thank you!"

Hok grinned. "You are welcome."

Bing looked at Seh and nodded. "Thanks are in order for you, too. I offer you my sincerest gratitude, young man."

Seh shrugged his shoulders. "I didn't do anything."

Bing stared, unblinking, at Seh. "It was your idea to wait for my daughter at the camp. You took a great risk. You should accept my thanks."

Seh looked embarrassed. He bowed toward Bing. "You are most welcome," he said. "I was very glad to sense Hok's *chi* outside the tent. Her *chi* is a lot like yours." Seh turned to Hok and bowed. "I . . . *we* . . . missed you."

Hok returned the bow, now embarrassed herself to be bowing so formally to her brother. She was about to thank Seh when she noticed Charles growing tense. Hok glanced at Charles, but he looked away, his pale cheeks turning red.

Fu growled softly, and Hok saw that Fu was staring at Charles. Fu must have noticed Charles' reaction, too. Was Charles . . . jealous?

Mong chuckled. "I see you have a couple of very protective brothers, Hok. One that will do anything to find you, and another that will defend your honor. That is good."

Hok blushed and looked down. Out of the corner of her eye, she noticed a strange movement. She glanced at Seh's sleeve and saw a snake's head poking out! She pointed to it. "What is *that*?"

"Just a friend," Seh said. "Would you like to pet it?" He reached his arm out toward Hok and she recoiled. Seh smirked.

"That was mean," Hok said. "You know how much I dislike snakes."

"Oh, well, thanks a lot," Seh the "snake" said in a joking tone.

"Yes, thanks a lot," Mong the "python" added. He winked.



Hok blushed even more.

"That's enough fun for now," Mong said. "Let's get down to business. What happened to you, Hok? Are you okay?"

"I'm fine," Hok replied. "I went to see Ying. I . . . helped him escape."

"You did WHAT!" Fu roared.

"Quiet!" Mong said, glaring at Fu. "Do you want to get us captured?"

Fu bit his lip and lowered his head. "Sorry," he mumbled.

"I am sorry, too," Hok said. "It felt like the right thing to do at the time, but now I'm not sure."

"What happened?" Bing asked.

"I made a deal with him," Hok said. "I knocked

out his guard—a general named Tsung—and released Ying. In return, Ying told me where we might find Malao."

"You knocked out Tsung?" Mong said. He smiled. "Your kung fu must be exceptional. I'm sorry I missed it. You now need to be more wary than ever, you know. Tsung will hunt you down."

Hok nodded. "I understand. Ying thought we should have killed him."

"You probably should have listened to Ying," Mong said. "No matter now. What's done is done. What did Ying have to say about Malao?"

"Ying told me about a small shack downstream from Kaifeng that he once used as a safe house. He says it's about an hour away and thinks Tonglong may have taken Malao there."

Mong nodded. "I always suspected Ying had a hideout somewhere along the Yellow River. I don't know much about Tonglong, but I wouldn't put it past him to try to use Malao as bait to obtain the map scroll from you. He's probably already planning a trap. You'll have to be careful."

Hok's thin eyebrows raised. "Be careful?"

"Your brother Malao needs you," Bing said. "You must go to him."

Mong walked around the table to where the dark-skinned girl was sitting and placed one of his enormous pale hands on her shoulder. She twisted her head up and grinned at him.

"This young woman is called Sum," Mong said.

"She and her twin brother, Cheen, lived at the stronghold with us, and they followed me and my colleagues here to Kaifeng after Ying and Tonglong overcame us. She and her brother are as at home in the water as they are on land. Neither of them speaks and we don't know their names, so we've taken to calling them Sum and Cheen, *Shallow* and *Deep.* I saw them both in the water yesterday when Malao was captured, and we came to this boathouse as soon as the soldiers left the Jade Phoenix because I knew Sum and Cheen have been living here. Sum was waiting for us, and from her gestures we believe her brother has followed Tonglong's boat. She wants to take us to locate her brother, and find Malao." Mong nodded toward the skiff.



"Sum wants to travel by *boat*?" Seh said. He swallowed hard.

Hok remembered that Seh hated boats. In fact, he disliked water in general. He wasn't a very good swimmer.

"A boat makes the most sense," Mong said. "It's the quickest way to get down the river. If you hurry, you might be able to surprise them."

Hok nodded and looked at Charles. This time, Charles held her gaze.

"My job is to stay here with your mother and GongJee," Charles said. "I'd like to help you, but I must stay. I'm sorry."

"I understand," Hok said. "Thank you for helping my family."

Charles blushed again.

"You can count me in," said Fu with a low growl.

"Me too," Seh added.

Sum nodded to Hok, and Hok nodded back.

Hok looked at Mong. "I guess that makes Fu, Seh, Sum, and me."

"Excellent," Mong said. "The four of you should fit in the skiff with enough room for Malao on the return trip. I suggest you leave immediately. With any luck, you'll be back by tomorrow. Someone will be waiting here for you."

Hok straightened up. She realized that if something were to go wrong, she might not see her mother again for some time. Bing seemed to read her mind.

"We shall see each other again," Bing said. "Soon."

"Yes," Hok replied. "Soon." She bowed to her mother, and her mother stood and bowed back, low and deep. Hok knew that a mother could not give her daughter a greater sign of respect.

"Let's get you four moving," Mong said.

# CHAPTER 16

Hok, Seh, and Fu spent the next two hours hiding beneath a moldy tarp on the floor of the skiff. They peeked out occasionally, peering at the southern shore through the heavy midmorning rain. Sum stood at the back of the boat, steadily poling it downstream.

The stretch of river they were currently on was strangely devoid of people. They hadn't seen another boat in quite a while, and they hadn't seen any buildings for more than an hour. Hok was considering closing her eyes to take a little break when Fu spotted something with his keen vision.

"There!" Fu whispered, poking one finger out from under the tarp. "A dragon boat."

Hok strained her eyes. Soon she saw it, too. A boat

had been pulled up onto the bank beneath a huge willow tree with twin trunks. The boat, and the trunks, were barely visible through the thick wall of leaves and pouring rain. This was the place.

The skiff turned toward the willow, and Seh tensed beside Hok. "What is Sum doing?" Seh whispered. "We shouldn't head straight for shore here. It might be a trap."

Fu swiveled his large head left, then right. "I don't think it's a trap. The closest line of cover is hundreds of paces away. There aren't any ambush points."

Hok scanned the shore. "I think Fu is right. Tonglong's men probably just put their boat under the tree to keep it from filling with rainwater. Or maybe they're trying to hide it. If Fu hadn't pointed it out, I don't think I would have even noticed it. The willow leaves hang all the way down to the water's surface."

"That's a poor hiding place," Seh said. "I have a bad feeling about this. My snake seems uneasy, too. What about the tree itself? Maybe there's somebody hiding in it."

"No," Fu replied, scanning the tree, top to bottom. "It's empty."

"Well, just in case," Seh said, "I think we should continue farther downstream and then sneak back up along the shore on foot."

"Well, I say we go straight to shore and take cover beneath that tree," Fu said. "I've got to get out from under this rotting tarp. It smells worse than Malao's feet. Do you sense anyone?"

"I'm not sure," Seh replied. "It's difficult to focus right now. The rain is distracting me. We need to get a little closer."

As the skiff continued toward the willow, Hok glanced back at Sum. She expected to see Sum watching the river in front of the boat. Instead, Sum was staring intently off the rear of the skiff. Hok followed Sum's gaze and noticed a thin stick drifting toward them. It floated upright, with one end poking out of the water. Also, it was moving *against* the current.

Seh and Fu must have noticed, too. Hok heard Seh hiss softly and Fu begin to growl. Fu's growling intensified when the stick suddenly disappeared beneath the surface.

A moment later, a teenage boy's head rose from the murky water directly behind the skiff. He had a long hollow stick in his teeth. He locked eyes with Sum, and a huge grin spread across his curiously flat face. Sum returned the smile. There was no question that the boy in the water was Sum's brother, Cheen. He had been using the stick to breathe while approaching underwater. Seh and Fu immediately relaxed.

Cheen pointed down the river, along the southern shore. He raised one hand out of the water and sketched a simple building in the air with one finger, then began to scratch one armpit like a monkey.

"Malao!" Fu said, and stood, pushing the tarp back. "Let's go and—"

Seh grabbed Fu's arm and jerked him toward the floor. The shallow skiff rocked violently. "Get down, Pussycat!" Seh whispered. "What if someone sees you?"

"There's no one out there," Fu growled.

"You don't know that," Seh said.

"No," Fu replied. "We're almost to the shore and nothing's happened yet. That means Tonglong and his men are probably huddled in the shack in front of a warm fire. They won't expect us to be traveling in weather like this. Let's go get them!"

"We need more information first," Seh hissed.

Hok glanced toward the riverbank. Fu was probably right, but a little more information couldn't hurt, either. Hok knew that Cheen and Sum didn't speak, so she tried to think of a question Cheen might be able to answer without words. "How many people are with Malao?"

Cheen raised three fingers.

Seh looked at Hok and his eyebrows raised. "That's good to know," Seh said. "Tonglong must have sent the soldiers back upstream to look for us. The three are probably Tonglong, AnGangseh, and HaMo."

Cheen nodded.

"I like these odds," Fu said. "There are five of us and only three of them. Let's get them!"

Cheen and Sum nodded as if in agreement, then froze. Something was wrong.

They reached the willow tree, and the front of the

skiff brushed against the low-hanging branches before passing beneath them. Hok ducked as the branches neared her head, and off the back of the boat she saw Cheen dive beneath the surface of the water and swim away. Sum dropped to her knees and gripped the sides of the skiff, staring straight ahead.

Puzzled, Hok turned toward shore as her body passed beneath the low-hanging willow leaves. Beneath the tree's canopy, she saw a hollow stick poking up out of the water. It was right in front of the boat.

"Watch out!" Fu shouted, pointing toward the stick. He stood, and the bow of the skiff suddenly shot skyward. Hok was flung into the wall of willow leaves, and she managed to grab hold of one of the sinewy branches. It held her weight.



Hok found herself dangling above the river's surface in the pouring rain while her brothers sailed beyond the tree limbs. As Seh and Fu splashed down into the rain-swollen river behind her, she heard them yell out simultaneously, "HaMo!"

Hok ducked her head back under the tree's canopy and saw a large man in the water. He had single-handedly upended their skiff. He was fat but obviously very strong, and resembled an enormous frog or perhaps a river toad.

A very angry river toad.

# CHAPTER 17

"Now *there's* something you don't see every day," the fat man said to Hok. "A young crane dangling from a tree like a frightened monkey. Did you learn that technique from your little brother Malao?"

The fat man chuckled and stood. He had been on his knees in the river, hiding under the water. Hok realized that he was the same man she had seen at the front of Tonglong's dragon boat yesterday. He must be HaMo, or *Toad*. Muddy water flowed around his bulging midsection as he began to wade toward her.

Hok wished she had learned a few treetop monkey-style kung fu techniques from Malao. Malao would be very good at defending himself with his feet while hanging from his hands. Crane stylists, however, had no such techniques. Hok would have to improvise.

HaMo was two steps away from her when something exploded out of the water directly beneath her feet. Hok instinctively pulled her knees up to her chest and looked down. It was Cheen. Quick as an eel, he slammed his palms into HaMo's chest, but HaMo didn't budge.

Hok glanced behind HaMo and saw Sum surface in the shallow water. She began to pound on the back of HaMo's knees. However, HaMo's thick legs didn't buckle. It seemed he was not going to let himself be toppled backward, or in any other direction.

Fu roared and Hok leaned her head outside the willow's canopy. Fu was splashing toward them through the river and heavy rain. Hok saw their skiff upside down, hung up on several large rocks. It was empty. She had no idea where Seh had gone.

HaMo let out a tremendous *CROAK!*, and Hok ducked her head back under the canopy to see him squat into the water with Sum still behind him. HaMo's hands dropped straight down in front of him all the way to the river bottom, and he shifted his weight forward onto his arms.

"Sum!" Hok cried out. "Back away—"

But it was too late. HaMo unleashed both his legs straight back behind himself, striking Sum square in the hips. She was lifted out of the water and sent hurling through the air onto the riverbank. She slammed into the willow's twin trunks and her head snapped back, striking the tree with a hollow thud. Sum slumped to the ground.

Cheen let out a high-pitched shriek, and HaMo stood up. Cheen threw his entire body forward, slamming both his fists into HaMo's enormous belly. Hok knew that Cheen's double hammer-hand blow would have dropped any of her brothers or former teachers to their knees. However, HaMo's stomach absorbed the impact like pond water absorbs a thrown pebble. Ripples of fat radiated out from HaMo's midsection as he grabbed hold of Cheen's neck with his two thick hands and thrust Cheen's head deep into the muddy river.

Hok was about to drop into the water to help Cheen when Fu pushed his way through the wall of willow leaves. Fu glanced around, looking confused.

"Help him!" Hok said.

"Seh?" Fu asked.

"No! Cheen! Help Cheen!"

"Where's Seh?"

"Just help Cheen! I'll look for Seh."

Fu locked eyes with HaMo and seemed to understand. Fu sprang into action. He leaped out of chest-high water and splashed down next to HaMo, cocking a tiger-claw fist back to his ear.

Hok saw a mixture of concern and amusement wash across HaMo's face. HaMo released Cheen and took a step back, out of Fu's reach.

Cheen half stood, half slouched. Dirty liquid poured from his mouth in spurts like a broken fountain. He began to wobble toward his sister at the base of the tree.

Fu and HaMo stood waist-deep in the river, sizing each other up. Hok twisted around and scanned the river outside the willow's canopy again, looking for Seh. She squinted through the heavy rain and was shocked to see him far downriver, struggling to stay afloat. He had never been a strong swimmer, and he seemed preoccupied with keeping one arm out of the water. It was his snake.

Hok turned back to Fu. Fu and HaMo were slowly circling one another.

"Fu!" Hok said. "I have to go help Seh!"

"No problem," Fu replied. "I'll be right behind you. This won't take long."

HaMo chuckled and Hok released the branch. As she drifted down, she heard HaMo say, "I like your spirit, boy. Forget your sister, I'm taking you to LaoShu instead—"

Hok hit the cold, shallow water feetfirst and began to swim. *What did HaMo mean by that?* she wondered.

Hok pushed HaMo out of her mind and headed for Seh with long, powerful strokes. The chilly water gave her extra incentive to keep her body in motion.

When she was halfway to Seh, Hok caught movement out of the corner of her eye. On the shore she saw two figures running. One was heading toward Fu and HaMo, the other toward Seh.

Judging by the first person's extraordinarily long

ponytail braid, the one heading for Fu and HaMo was Tonglong. The other person was tiny by comparison and dressed from head to toe in black. A hood as dark as night kept the second person's face out of the heavy rain and out of Hok's sight, but Hok knew exactly who it was. It was Seh's mother, AnGangseh, or *Cobra*—the woman who had captured Malao the day before.

AnGangseh reached the water's edge downriver of Seh and waded in up to her waist. She reached into her sleeve and Hok thought that AnGangseh was going to pull out something to extend her reach in order to help Seh as he floundered in the water. Instead, AnGangseh's wrist snapped powerfully outward in the direction of Seh's bobbing head.

Even under the darkened skies and pouring rain, Hok saw the flash of metal sink into Seh's neck. He choked loud enough for Hok to hear, and his body went limp in the water.

"No!" Hok cried. It was a throwing dart, and judging by Seh's reaction, Hok was certain it had been tipped with poison.

Hok began to swim furiously toward Seh. Behind her, she heard Fu roar—and then stop.

"No! No! No!" Hok shouted. Whatever had just happened to Fu had knocked *him* out, or worse.

Hok slowed in the water and raised her head toward AnGangseh. AnGangseh threw back her black hood and flashed a deadly beautiful smile at Hok as Seh drifted into her arms.

Hok was powerless to help. AnGangseh reached into Seh's robe and removed the dragon scroll he carried. She slipped the scroll up her sleeve and did the unthinkable.

Still staring at Hok, AnGangseh flipped Seh facedown in the river and shoved him into the current. Then she turned up her hood and slithered back to shore.

# CHAPTER 18

Hok could not believe what she had just seen. She wished it was another bad dream but knew this was not the case. Seh was going to die.

Hok spread her arms wide and thrust them deep into the cold, muddy river, propelling herself forward at a frantic pace. Ahead of her in the darkness and pouring rain, Seh's unconscious body convulsed and rolled over in the river's current. At least he was now floating faceup. She might have a chance to save him.

Hok reached Seh and slipped behind him. She wrapped her arms around his chest, kicking her feet powerfully to keep both their heads above water. She leaned her head over Seh's shoulder and placed her ear in front of his lips. At the same time, she squeezed his narrow rib cage, hoping to hear something telling.

Hok got more than an earful.

Seh suddenly retched, a thick stream of dirty river water and stomach bile spewing out of his mouth. Hok shuddered and shook her head. She tilted her face toward the sky and let the heavy rain wash her skin clean. Through her arms, Hok felt Seh's chest heaving. He was breathing.

However, Seh was still very much unconscious. Hok would have to swim for both of them. With one arm around her brother and the other arm—her injured arm—paddling with all her might, Hok began to slowly make her way toward the shore.

With her good arm around Seh's chest, Hok felt something wriggle beneath his collar. It was his snake. She had forgotten all about it. Hok fought the urge to pull her arm away and shifted her grip. The snake's colorful head poked out of Seh's collar, into the rain-soaked gloom.

Hok turned away. She glanced back upstream and her eyes widened. Tonglong had pulled his dragon boat out beyond the willow's canopy and was launching it into the river! AnGangseh was with him.

Hok sank as low in the water as possible, pulling Seh and the snake down with her. They needed to find cover. Hok spotted a large tree leaning into the swollen river and made for it with every bit of strength she had left.

Hok reached the tree and its jumble of twisted limbs as Tonglong pushed the dragon boat out into the current with AnGangseh aboard. Hok slipped into the tangled mess with Seh in tow and locked one arm around him, the other around a thick, slippery limb. The current was much stronger here. If she wasn't careful, she and Seh would be washed out into the open.

The dragon boat raced downstream through the heavy rain with surprising speed. AnGangseh was at the bow, Tonglong at the stern. Each was rowing with a single paddle. Otherwise, the boat was empty. Soon they were close enough for Hok to hear them.

"Sssteer clear of that tree in the water," AnGangseh said, pointing to Hok's hiding place.

"But what if the girl is hiding in there?" Tonglong asked. "Or Seh?"

"Forget about them," AnGangseh said. "Ssseh is as good as dead, and the girl is no longer of value to us. HaMo is sssatisfied with the monkey and tiger boys as payment. Those boys will earn him a fortune. We have what we desire, and it isn't worth our time to capture the girl and turn her in to the authorities. We need to make haste."

"Then make haste we shall," Tonglong replied.

And just like that, the dragon boat passed.

Hok sighed with relief. She looked at Seh still locked under her arm. *How could a mother talk about her son that way?* she wondered.

Hok took a few moments to catch her breath, and her mind began to race. *What was HaMo going to do with Malao and Fu?* she wondered. *Turn them in for the reward she'd seen posted in Kaifeng?* At least they were still alive—for now.

Hok began to shiver in the chilly water, and she decided to get moving. She shoved herself clear of the tangled tree limbs and gave Seh a tug.

Seh didn't budge.

Hok tugged on Seh again. He remained anchored.

Hok looked closer and realized that one of Seh's feet was hung up on something. Try as she might, she couldn't get him free.

Hok wondered what she should do next. She was quickly running out of energy. All this swimming was taking its toll.

As if in response, Hok saw a second boat approaching through the darkness and heavy rain. It was Cheen on the skiff, scanning the shore.

*That's right,* Hok remembered. *The skiff had gotten hung up upstream. Cheen must have pulled it free and righted it. He's looking for us.*

Hok lifted herself as high as possible in the water and waved one arm while still holding on to Seh. Cheen saw her.

As Cheen pulled alongside the tree, Hok saw Sum, unconscious on the floor of the skiff. "I am happy to see you," Hok said. "My brother Seh is stuck. Would you please help?"

Cheen nodded and pointed to the shore. Hok knew exactly what he meant. He was going to run the skiff aground, then swim out to help. In no time, Cheen had done just that. When he reached Hok's side, he dove into the river's murky depths.

A moment later, Seh was free. Hok held on to him tightly and she began to swim as best she could toward the shore.

Cheen surfaced next to Hok and helped her get Seh onto the slippery riverbank. The rising river was quickly swallowing trees and eroding large chunks of the muddy shoreline. They wouldn't be safe there for long. Hok had to hurry.

Hok and Cheen laid Seh beneath a large oak, away from the water's edge, and Cheen went back to Sum, who was still unconscious in the skiff.

Hok needed to look at Seh's neck. She reached down to pull his collar back, and something stirred beneath it—his snake.

Hok jerked her hand away and grabbed a stick. She pushed Seh's soaking wet collar down and peered at his neck from several different angles. It looked like AnGangseh's poison dart hadn't sunk too deep. There was a small laceration, but the dart was not still embedded in the wound. This was good.

On the other hand, Hok was all too aware of potential complications from poison delivered by dart. A sticky residue was required to make the poison stick to the dart. That same sticky residue also made the poison stick to the wound. Hopefully, the river water and heavy rain had washed most of the poison away as soon as the dart struck.

In her mind's eye, Hok began to flip through a hundred different texts on poisons. She shook her head.

She was wasting her time. Even if she did manage

to identify the poison, she had no antidotes. The best she could do would be to scour the area for herbs to help counter any side effects, though even that would likely be of little help. The only way to administer treatments to an unconscious person was to make a tea from the necessary ingredients and pour it down a patient's throat. She had no way of making a fire. She didn't even have a pot to boil water in.

Hok sighed and looked toward Cheen. He was standing over the skiff with his head in his hands. Hok could tell that he was crying.

Hok walked over to the skiff and looked down at Sum. It would be much more difficult to tell what was wrong with her. Whenever anyone had suffered a similar injury at Cangzhen, they had always waited until the person regained consciousness before attempting any sort of diagnosis. She could try to wake Sum up with special pungent herbs, but she didn't have any with her.

Hok placed her hand softly on Cheen's shoulder. "Thank you for helping me with my brother. I wish there were something I could do for your sister. If I only had a medicine bag with me, I—"

Cheen's body went rigid and he snapped his head up. Hok saw a glimmer of hope in his eyes. He pointed downriver excitedly. Perhaps he knew where to find some herbs.

Cheen pointed to Seh and motioned for Hok to stay next to the skiff. Hok nodded and watched as Cheen ran beneath the oak tree, carefully lifted Seh, and carried him back to the boat. Cheen laid Seh inside the skiff next to his sister and motioned for Hok to help him push the skiff back into the river.

Hok glanced downriver and thought about Tonglong and AnGangseh. They were out there somewhere. HaMo was, too. AnGangseh had said that they weren't interested in her or Seh, but she couldn't be sure.

Hok ran her hands through her stubbly brown hair. Anything was better than standing around in the rain, watching the river rise. Besides, she had to at least try to treat Seh and Sum. Both might suffer long-term damage if left unattended, or even lose their lives.

Hok helped Cheen push the skiff back into the swollen river and climbed aboard.

# CHAPTER 19

Hok watched Cheen skillfully steer the skiff downstream for hours through the heavy rain. By late afternoon, she still hadn't seen any signs of Tonglong, AnGangseh, or HaMo. She hadn't seen any other boats venturing out in this horrible weather, period. The only thing she had seen was *li* after *li* of swamped trees, and great mounds of mud sliding down the riverbank into the river. The mud had an increasingly yellow tint, and Hok knew the color came from a special mineral, one used to make explosive powder. It was the abundance of this mineral that gave the river its name—the Yellow River.

*Horrible weapons, qiangs,* Hok thought, and her mind drifted to Charles. She wondered how he was doing. Hopefully, he hadn't had to use his weapons. She hoped he was still with her mother and GongJee and that they were all doing fine. Malao and Fu were another story. Hok simply hoped those two were alive. The same was true for her oldest brother, Long, who had essentially disappeared.

Hok looked at Seh, unconscious on the floor of the skiff. He was lying on his back with his face to one side, and she noticed a pool of rainwater accumulating near his nose. She bent over and rolled Seh onto his side to get his face out of the puddle, and her thin eyebrows raised up. There was a long, narrow bulge in the small of Seh's back that she hadn't noticed before. In some ways, it resembled the outline of one of Charles' *qiangs*. Also, tied to one side of Seh's sash was a pouch. Hok poked the pouch and it jingled. There were coins inside. She wondered where he had gotten money.

Hok reached toward the bulge in Seh's back, then jerked her hand away. A telltale lump on Seh's right wrist began to move. It was his snake. She would have to work quickly if she wanted to find out what Seh was hiding.

Hok untied Seh's sash and rolled him gently onto his stomach. She took hold of the bottom of his blue silk robe and flipped it up. Tucked into the waist of Seh's silk pants was some sort of scroll. Even though it was thoroughly soaked, Hok could tell it wasn't one of the dragon scrolls. It looked too new to be something as old as the scrolls were supposed to be.

Hok stared at the scroll for a moment and noticed the snake beginning to make its way up Seh's arm, beneath his robe sleeve. Hok snatched the scroll away and folded Seh's robe back down. As the snake began to make its way over Seh's shoulder, she turned him back onto his back and quickly retied his sash.

The snake poked its head out of the folds of Seh's robe, and Hok leaned backward. The snake stared at her for a moment, then pulled its colorful head back into Seh's robe, out of the rain.

Hok shuddered and looked up. She saw Cheen staring at her.

"I don't like snakes very much," Hok said.

Cheen nodded as if in agreement and turned away, staring intently downstream. Hok noticed that his mood seemed to have changed. He appeared anxious.

"Are we close to our destination?" Hok asked.

Cheen nodded again. Less than half an hour later, he pointed toward shore. Hok squinted through the rain and saw a small house set back in the trees atop a mound of yellow earth. It was a simple wooden structure, wisely built quite some distance from the rising water.

Cheen steered the skiff toward the shore and found a narrow clearing between two partially submerged maple trees. He ran the skiff up onto a stretch of yellow mud and jumped out. Hok followed. Together they dragged the skiff into the forest, well beyond the water's edge.

Cheen scooped up his sister and nodded for Hok

to do the same with Seh. Leery of the snake, Hok cradled Seh in her arms like a baby instead of slinging him over her shoulder like she would normally have done. Holding Seh this way was difficult, to say the least, especially with her arm still hurting, but at least she could keep an eye on the undulating lump that had once again settled around Seh's wrist.

Cheen headed for the house with Hok on his heels. They reached the front door and Cheen knocked against it with one foot. No one answered.

Cheen knocked again, a little harder this time, and the door swung inward. He walked straight into the house without announcing them. Hok followed warily, her eyes darting left to right.

The moment Hok crossed the threshold, she relaxed. There were herbs everywhere! They hung from the walls and the ceiling. Piles were stacked on the floor. Hok saw cabinets and bottles and buckets and barrels overflowing with medicinal plants. She could tell that this was the home of a doctor. More than likely, a very good doctor.

Hok saw numerous things that she could use to help Seh once he regained consciousness. Why, right next to the door was a row of lung-enhancing herbs. There were huge clumps of *hai zao,* or seaweed; large pots of *xing ren,* or apricot kernels; small jars of *bai jie zi,* or mustard seeds . . . the list was endless. Hok realized that there were more herbs here than they had ever had back at Cangzhen. There were even a few she couldn't identify.

Excited, Hok set Seh down on the earthen floor to

take a better look around. As she did, she noticed the snake on Seh's arm go rigid.

Hok heard a voice behind her.

"Can I help you?"

Hok turned to see an ancient woman hunched over in the doorway. Her wet hair was thin and gray, but her skin was taut and her eyes shined bright and clear. She was very old, but appeared extraordinarily healthy.

Hok lowered her head. She felt like a thief. "I—"

"CHEEN!" the old woman exclaimed suddenly, interrupting Hok. "Is that you? I haven't seen you in ages! Come over here so that I can get a good look at you."

Cheen approached the old woman with Sum in his arms. The old woman's face went pale.

"Oh, dear," she said. She glanced at Seh lying on the floor, then her eyes settled on Hok. "You poor children. My name is PawPaw. You have come to the right place. I am a healer."

Hok felt the warm glow of relief spread through her soaking wet body. *PawPaw* meant *Grandmother.* What a perfect name for a healer.

Hok wiped the rain from her brow and bowed. "My name is Hok."

"A pleasure to meet you, Hok," PawPaw said with a polite nod. "It is a shame we couldn't have met under better circumstances. Who did this to you?"

"A man called Tonglong, a man called HaMo, and a woman called AnGangseh," Hok answered.

PawPaw spat. "You must be pretty special to have

the likes of them on your tail. I will do what I can to help you. Cheen and Sum have helped me several times in the past. You seemed to be looking for something a moment ago. What was it?"

"*Xiang mu*," Hok replied.

PawPaw looked surprised.

"It's a type of evergreen tree," Hok said. "But it has leaves. It's medicinal."

"I know what it is," PawPaw said. "Do you prefer the leaves, the stem, or the bark?"

"It depends how fresh the clippings are," Hok said. "What I'm really looking for is salve squeezed from fresh-cut branches."

PawPaw's eyebrows raised. "What will you do with it? Have them drink it?"

"Never!" Hok said. "I want to rub a bit beneath their noses to see if the smell will wake them up."

PawPaw smiled. "I see you have a talent for the healing arts, yet you are still quite young. I am impressed. I would have prescribed the exact same thing. Unfortunately, I do not have what you need, but I know where you can find a healthy specimen. There is a village nearby, and the tree you seek grows in its central courtyard. It is a bit of a walk, but I will take you there. Let's get Sum and your friend comfortable first."

"His name is Seh," Hok offered as she bent over and picked Seh up again.

"Snake and Crane?" PawPaw said. "That's odd. The two animals usually don't get along."

"He is my brother," Hok said.

"I see," PawPaw said. "Bring your brother in here, then." She headed into the next room.

Hok followed and found herself in a small bedroom with two narrow beds. PawPaw pointed to one. "Place Seh there," she said. Cheen entered the bedroom and laid Sum down on the other one.

"What is wrong with them?" PawPaw asked.

"Sum hit her head very hard against a tree," Hok replied. "Seh was struck in the neck with a poisoned dart."

"When did this happen?"

"Several hours ago," Hok said.

"Then there isn't anything we can do for either of them," PawPaw said. "What's done is done. We'll have to wait for them to wake up." She looked at Cheen. "Can you keep an eye on these unfortunate souls while Hok and I go to the village?"

Cheen nodded.

"Good," PawPaw said. She nodded toward a large trunk in one corner of the room. "You'll find several dry robes in there, Cheen. Get yourself out of those wet clothes, and change Seh's and Sum's clothes as well. Are you comfortable doing that?"

Cheen nodded again.

"All right, then," PawPaw said. "Come with me, Hok. I have the perfect outfit for you to wear when we return. For now, you might as well just stay in those wet clothes. We're going to get soaked walking to the village."

PawPaw walked out of the bedroom and turned

suddenly toward the open front door. Hok thought PawPaw was getting ready to leave, but then Hok heard footsteps splashing outside. A rain-soaked boy raced up to the doorway and collapsed against it, completely out of breath. He looked like he had been running for quite some time. He closed his eyes and bent over, his hands on his knees, as Hok stepped out of the bedroom.

"The village . . . ," the boy managed to say between breaths, ". . . was attacked. . . . Please . . . come help. . . . Bring your . . . medicines."

"Attacked?" PawPaw replied as she began to scramble, grabbing a wide variety of items and throwing them into a large basket. "Tell me more."

"It was . . . the Emperor's . . . soldiers," the boy said as he sucked wind.

"Are you sure?" PawPaw asked. "Why on earth would the Emperor's men bother to attack a small village in the middle of nowhere?"

"They said . . . they were looking for . . . someone . . . important."

"That's preposterous," PawPaw said. "Who on earth could be that important?"

The boy opened his eyes and glanced around the room. When his gaze met Hok's, a terrible scowl settled across his face.

"They were looking for . . . a traitor. . . . A girl . . . with brown hair. . . ."

# CHAPTER 20

Hok could hardly believe her ears. Was an entire village really attacked because of her?

The boy in the doorway straightened up and took a step toward Hok, still scowling.

"Stop right there," PawPaw said. "You will not lay a hand on her. There has been enough violence today."

Behind her in the bedroom, Hok heard a noise. She looked over her shoulder and saw Cheen puff out his chest. He walked to her side and stared hard at the boy.

Hok hardly knew what to say. She didn't want anyone to fight over her, and she felt horrible about the attack. She looked at the boy. "I am very sorry about your village. I am not a bad person. Let me prove it. I will help heal your wounded."

The boy continued to scowl. "You can't help us! This is all your fault. Besides, you're just a girl."

PawPaw looked the boy in the eye. "Listen to me, young man. I believe this girl has done nothing wrong. She has proven to be an experienced healer, and she can help your fellow villagers. I suggest you let her help. I also suggest you keep your mouth shut about who you think she might be."

The boy's eyes narrowed and he folded his arms.

"Let me put it this way," PawPaw said. "If she doesn't go, I don't go. The fate of your village lies in your hands."

Anxiety filled the boy's eyes. "Okay," he said. "I won't tell. Please, hurry!"

"Good," PawPaw said. She opened a cabinet drawer and removed a straight razor. She handed it to Hok.

Hok was dumbfounded. "A weapon?" she asked.

"By the heavens, no," PawPaw said. "It's for your head. You can't go looking the way you do. Even if I had a large hat or turban to cover your brown hair, there are still risks. You must shave it off. You need to change your clothes, too. You'll have to pretend to be a boy."

Hok frowned. "I understand. What about Sum and Seh? Won't we be gone for a while?"

"They could be asleep for a day or more," PawPaw replied. "Come, help me now at the village and I promise I will do everything I can for Sum and your brother when we return. The four of you can stay with me until Sum and Seh make full recoveries."

Hok hesitated, then nodded.

PawPaw turned to Cheen. "There should be a boy's robe and pants in that trunk I showed you that Hok can wear. Could you please find them for her?"

Cheen nodded and headed for the other room.

PawPaw looked at Hok. "Behind the house you will find a rain barrel. Shave your head, then come back in and change. I will finish gathering the necessary items. Hurry!"

While they raced as quickly as possible, in the heavy rain, it still took them more than half an hour to reach the village by foot. PawPaw had said the river was too swollen and treacherous to attempt to travel by boat.



As they approached, it was clear the soldiers had already left. The scene reminded Hok of Cangzhen and Shaolin. She wondered how people could be so cruel to one another.

The village was large by local standards, but it was nowhere near as big as Kaifeng. Hok saw perhaps one hundred buildings of various sizes, and several of them were smoldering in the rain. They passed by rows of storefronts riddled with holes from *qiangs* on their way to the central square.

Once they reached the square, Hok immediately identified the *xiang mu* tree that PawPaw had mentioned. Hok thought about how she might use it to wake Seh, but that thought only lasted a moment.

Once the villagers realized that PawPaw had arrived, Hok and PawPaw were overrun with injured people of all ages.

A group of men quickly set up a small tent, and Hok and PawPaw set up their makeshift clinic inside it. Hundreds of injured villagers lined up outside in the fading afternoon light, shivering in the cold rain. By the time night had fallen, the rain had mercifully ceased. Several large fires were started to help chase away the chill for those still awaiting treatment, and oil lanterns were brought into the tent to work by. It was a very long night.

Most of the wounds Hok saw were from *qiangs*, and they were unlike any she had treated previously. Weapons-practice mishaps were fairly common at Cangzhen, and she had gotten quite good at dealing with those types of injuries. While a sword or spear could slice flesh and cause blood loss, the wound could be treated in a rather straightforward and obvious manner. The wounds simply needed to be wrapped tightly and the dressings changed often.

*Qiang* wounds, on the other hand, required much more skilled attention. The lead balls fired from a *qiang* left gaping holes in the skin that could not be closed by simply realigning the remaining sections of flesh. The holes had to be filled, and clean packing material was in short supply. Additionally, the *qiang* balls shattered bone, crippling the victim and leaving fragments that needed to be removed. Fragments of bone could lead to infection.

Unfortunately, Hok also encountered a few patients who were beyond help. Hok tried her best to make them as comfortable as possible, using any means she could think of. In some cases, that meant Dream Dust. PawPaw kept a small supply, and Hok let her administer it. Hok wanted nothing to do with it.

By the time Hok had seen the last patient, the sun was rising and she was so tired, she could barely keep her eyes open. PawPaw came over and handed her a piece of ginseng root to chew on for energy.

"You did very well last night," PawPaw said. "I would say that you will make a great healer one day, but I believe you already are one. Thank you."

Hok frowned. "Don't thank me. It was my fault that—"

PawPaw raised her hand. "I don't want to hear any more of that kind of talk." She glanced around and lowered her voice. "Let me tell you a secret. I communicate with a man called NgGung who possesses vast amounts of information about people and events in this region. I know who you are and I believe you've done nothing wrong."

Hok blinked. "I've met him," she said.

"Wonderful!" PawPaw said with a smile. "Then there is nothing more to discuss on this topic. What we haven't discussed yet is what you plan to do next. What do you have in mind?"

Hok rubbed her tired eyes. "I'd like to stay here. These people need treatment. So does Seh."

"But what about your other brothers?" PawPaw asked. "NgGung told me you had a total of four brothers who survived the attack against Cangzhen. Haven't you made plans with them?"

Hok shook her head. "I don't even know where they are anymore, except for Seh, and I don't expect he'll be fit to travel for several weeks at least. Until then, I think I can help the most people by staying here. After that, I'll go in search of my brothers with Seh."

PawPaw smiled. "That is very thoughtful of you, helping the majority. These villagers will never forget your selflessness. I suggest you stay with me until enough people recover to the point that I can handle the remaining treatments myself. We should reach that point about the same time your brother Seh is fit enough to travel. How does that sound?"

Hok thought more about Seh and frowned. "Do you think Seh will recover completely? And what about Sum?"

"Honestly, I think they will both be fine," PawPaw said. "Sum will wake to a terrible headache that will last a few days, but it will wear off. As for Seh, he is young and appears fit. His body is waging war against the poison as we speak. There is only one sure way to verify Seh's condition, though, and that is to wake him. Come, let us gather the necessary ingredients and go to him now."

PawPaw pulled a small knife from her basket and handed it to Hok. Hok collected several branches from the *xiang mu* tree hanging over their heads, and they left for PawPaw's house.

# CHAPTER 21

Less than an hour later, Hok and PawPaw arrived at PawPaw's home. They were greeted with a pleasant surprise. Sum was awake.

Sum and Cheen sat beside one another on Sum's bed in PawPaw's bedroom. On the other bed, Seh still lay unconscious. Hok was happy about Sum, but worried about Seh.

PawPaw walked over to Sum and took hold of her left wrist. "Are you feeling all right?"

Sum smiled weakly and nodded. She slowly turned her head and pointed to the back of it. There was a large lump and a bit of dried blood in her short black hair.

PawPaw released Sum's left wrist and grabbed the

right. Hok knew that PawPaw was checking Sum's various pulses. At the same time, PawPaw stared deep into Sum's eyes, looking for signs of concussion.

PawPaw let go of Sum's wrist and leaned back. "Except for a big headache, I think you'll be just fine." PawPaw pointed to Seh. "Has he woken?"

Cheen shook his head.

"I was afraid of that," PawPaw said. She turned to Hok. "Would you like to try and wake him, or should I?"

"I'll do it," Hok replied, and she got right to work. She knelt next to Seh and reached into PawPaw's basket, removing the knife and a section of *xiang mu* branch. She made several deep cuts in the branch and twisted it round and round upon itself. Drops of pungent liquid formed along the slices. Hok's eyes began to water from the acrid fumes.

Hok blinked several times and wiped one finger along the length of the *xiang mu* branch, then dabbed it on Seh's upper lip directly below his nostrils.

Seh's body jerked, and his eyes flew open. He lifted his head, then swooned and lay back down, his eyes closed.

"Hok?" Seh muttered. "Is that you?"

"Yes," Hok said. "We are in the home of a healer. Her name is PawPaw. How do you feel?"

"Awful," Seh replied.

Hok reached out and took Seh's hand. "You were poisoned. You are lucky to be alive."

Seh took a deep breath, and Hok saw tears forming in the corners of his closed eyes. "I remember," he said.

PawPaw cleared her throat. "Why don't we let your brother rest awhile? I'll come back and give you a thorough examination later, Seh."

"Yes . . . ," Seh replied. "I'd like to be alone."

Hok wasn't surprised.

"Have a good nap, then," PawPaw said. She stood and left the room. Cheen helped Sum stand, and they followed PawPaw out.

Hok let go of Seh's hand. "I'll come back later, too. If you still want to be alone then, just let me know."

Seh nodded and Hok left the room. She found PawPaw waiting for her.



"So, what do you think?" PawPaw asked.

"Considering what he's been through," Hok said, "I think he looks good."

"I'd have to agree," PawPaw said. "That is why I didn't bother to poke and prod him just yet. I was concerned that he might have suffered some sort of paralysis, but he lifted his head when he spoke and he gripped your hand. I also saw his toes move."

"Paralysis?" Hok said. "I never thought of that."

"Depending on the poison used," PawPaw said, "there could have been permanent damage to the pathways that carry signals to certain parts of his body, particularly to the internal organs and limbs. This is especially true if the poison came from a venom as opposed to a plant."

“I suppose AnGangseh could have used a venom-based poison,” Hok said.

“Exactly,” PawPaw replied. “After all, her name does mean *Cobra* in Cantonese. She probably wanted to immobilize him.”

Hok nodded. She thought about sharing what little she knew about AnGangseh, especially the part about AnGangseh being Seh’s mother. In the end, though, Hok thought better of it. If Seh wanted his secrets shared, he should be the one to do it.

Hok rubbed her eyes. She was exhausted.

“Let’s get some rest ourselves,” PawPaw said. “When we wake up, I’ll make us some rice and a nice pot of ginseng soup. We’ll need all the energy we can get. We have a lot of work ahead of us.”

Over the next several weeks, Hok and PawPaw established a routine. Each morning they would travel to the village to check on the scores of patients, and each evening they would return to PawPaw’s house. Hok kept her head clean-shaven and continued to wear the clothes PawPaw had given her the first day. The outfit was a lightweight gray peasant’s robe and pants that fit Hok well and suited the increasingly warm weather.

In some ways, Hok’s life at PawPaw’s house reminded her of her life at Cangzhen. While she didn’t particularly enjoy pretending to be something she wasn’t—a boy—at least life was relatively peaceful here. She worked hard with PawPaw, but she had always worked hard at Cangzhen, too.

Meanwhile, Seh slowly began to recover, though he had not yet gotten strong enough to leave his bed. Sum was recovering much quicker, and she and Cheen spent much of their time fishing on the slowly receding river and keeping an eye on Seh. Hok wished she could spend more time with Seh, but she was gone all day and exhausted at night. The few times she did try and talk with him, he shooed her away or pretended to be tired. She assumed he was upset that she was gone so much. She didn't blame him.

In time, the number of village patients decreased to where Hok only needed to be in the village a few hours each day. However, she was busier than ever. She spent any remaining daylight and often some of the night roaming the surrounding forest with PawPaw, collecting herbs and berries and other medicines to replenish PawPaw's severely depleted stockpile. Hok tried a few times to convince Seh to join them, but he was never interested. PawPaw said that Seh was now able to walk around, but Hok had only ever seen him in bed with his eyes closed and a pout on his face.

There was a point when Hok thought Seh's downhearted mood had to do with his snake. She'd seen it slither out of the house on more than one occasion. However, it always returned, usually with a rodent-shaped lump in its midsection.

Hok began to worry about Seh. While his physical health had improved greatly, his mental state appeared to be deteriorating. He was growing increasingly moody, and often said things that were downright mean if Hok asked to examine him. He would only let PawPaw attend to him, and Hok felt that her brother was beginning to slip away from her. While they had never been extremely close at Cangzhen, they had a strong mutual respect that Hok had always felt, partially because Seh had known that she was a girl but had concealed it from everyone.

Hok felt that that respect was now gone, and it bothered her. She used to think that he was upset that she spent so little time with him, but now she was certain there was more to it. She wanted to know if she had said or done something to cause this. Or perhaps his behavior was just an unfortunate side effect of the poison. Regardless, Hok needed to know if she could remedy the situation. She decided to talk to Seh about it.

The next morning, Cheen and Sum left to go fishing, and PawPaw was outside laying herbs to dry in the sun. Hok went into the back room and, as usual, found Seh lying facedown. "I'd like to talk with you," she said.

Seh didn't reply.

Hok knelt on the floor, next to Seh's head. "I'm worried about you, Seh. You seem depressed."

"I'm fine."

"I don't think so," Hok said. "PawPaw told me that she was going to add some wild date seeds and young rose flower to your daily teas to help strengthen your spirits. Has she?"

"I don't know," Seh replied. "I stopped asking the ingredients long ago."

"That's funny," Hok said. "The Seh I know was always very curious. He would never consume anything without knowing exactly what was in it."

"Perhaps the Seh you know is gone," he replied. "Perhaps he was left back at the river. Why don't you go look for him? Just leave me alone."

Hok shook her head. She decided to try another approach. She stood and walked over to one corner of the room. Hidden under a stack of baskets was the scroll she had recovered from the small of Seh's back after he had been poisoned. She retrieved it and returned to Seh's side.

"I almost forgot about this," Hok said, unrolling the scroll. "What is it?"



"What does it look like?" Seh said without looking up.

"A dragon scroll, I suppose. Except the writing looks very hurried and the parchment does not seem old. There is a sketch of human *chi* meridians on one side and a pressure-point sketch on the other."

"It's a *copy* of a dragon scroll," Seh said. "I made it when you were off breaking Ying out of jail."

"Oh," Hok said. "Copying the original was a very clever thing to do."

Seh didn't reply.

Hok thought about what Seh had just said about breaking Ying out of jail. "Are you upset that I helped Ying escape?"

"No."

Hok paused and took a deep breath. "Are you . . . upset about your mother?"

"I don't want to talk about it."

"Well, I think you *should* talk about it," Hok said. "Maybe it will make you feel better."

"I doubt it," Seh replied.

"How do you know unless you try?" Hok said.

"No."

Hok sighed. This wasn't working. She decided to try one last approach. She unrolled the dragon scroll further. "What do you think is so special about this scroll? It doesn't look very special."

"It's a map," Seh said.

Hok blinked. "A map? Are you sure?"

"Yes," Seh replied.

"I don't see how—"

"Don't look *at* it," Seh snapped. "Hold it up to the light and look *through* it. The lines on the two sketches merge and form a map."

Hok stared at the sketches. "What is it a map of?"

"I don't know."

Hok stared some more. She saw what Seh was talking about, but she played ignorant in order to try and get Seh to open up to her. "I don't see what you're talking about," she said. "Can you show me?"

"No."

"Please?"

"No!"

"What's wrong with you, Seh? Why won't you show me?"

"I don't want to."

"But—"

"No!" Seh shouted. "Leave me alone!"

Hok lowered the scroll and stared at Seh.

"Hok?" PawPaw called from outside the house. "Could you come here for a moment?"

"I'll be right there," Hok called back. She looked at Seh. "I am sorry if I upset you, Seh, but I still think we need to talk. I'm leaving now, but I'll be back."

Seh didn't respond.

Hok placed the scroll next to Seh and walked outside. She found PawPaw some distance away.

"There is something wrong with him," Hok said. "Isn't there?"

"Yes," PawPaw replied. "There is no point in hiding it any longer. I overheard some of your conversation, and your diagnosis that he is depressed is correct. He has been taking both wild date seeds and young rose flower, but I'm afraid all the seeds and flowers in the world will not help him."

Hok's eyes widened. "Is it serious?"

"Very serious," PawPaw said. "As you know, Seh is quite secretive. He didn't want anyone to know about his condition, and because of his extraordinary sensitivity to *chi* and other things, he's been able to function extremely well. However, once he leaves my home he will no longer be able to hide his condition from you. I am surprised he's been able to hide it this long. He should have told you himself by now, but it seems his secrecy continues to get the best of him. If you hadn't been so preoccupied, you would have surely noticed."

"What is wrong with him?" Hok asked, her voice beginning to tremble.

"Remember when we discussed the possibility that Seh might suffer paralysis as a result of being poisoned?"

"Yes . . ."

"Well, it seems my concerns were justified."

"But you said weeks ago that he wasn't paralyzed," Hok said. "I've seen him move just about every part of his body myself."

"Remember I said that there was the possibility of damage to the pathways that carry signals to certain parts of the body?" PawPaw asked. "In Seh's case, it seems the channel that feeds his eyes was permanently damaged by the poison."

Hok stared at her, confused.

"Hok," PawPaw said, "Seh is blind."

# CHAPTER 22

Later that evening, Hok stood over Seh's bed, staring at his closed eyes. He was lying perfectly still and by all accounts appeared to be asleep. Hok, however, knew better. Seh was an excellent actor. She wanted to believe that Seh's acting skills were the reason she hadn't noticed his blindness, but deep down she knew that she simply hadn't paid enough attention to him. That was about to change.

"Hello, Seh," Hok said. "I'm back."

"I know," Seh replied, his eyes still closed. "I sensed you walk into the room. I also sensed you standing in the doorway forever. Don't do that again. It makes me uncomfortable, being stared at when I can't stare back."

Hok lowered her head. "I'm sorry. It sounds like you now know that I am aware of your . . . condition?"

"Yes," Seh grumbled. "I overheard you talking with PawPaw. My hearing is improving, you know. So is my sense of smell. Pretty soon, I'll be just like Fu, of all people. Funny, isn't it?"

"I don't find it funny at all," Hok said. "Your body is adjusting. It's helping you cope."

"Well, I could do without that kind of help, or any other kind," Seh said. "That is why you are here now, isn't it? To offer to help me?"

"Yes," Hok said. "You know how I am. PawPaw wants to help you, too. We've been talking and—"

"I can do without your help," Seh interrupted.

"But—"

"I said, *I can do without your help,*" Seh repeated. "What don't you understand?"

"I don't understand a lot of things," Hok replied. "Your situation is one of them, but I'm trying to learn."

"Well, go find yourself another teacher. Leave me alone."

Hok frowned. "Let me help you."

"Go away."

"No."

"Why won't you just leave me be?" Seh asked. "I'm not hurting anyone."

"You're hurting yourself," Hok said. "PawPaw thinks that you are severely depressed, and I agree. Especially listening to you now. PawPaw and I may not be able to do anything about your eyesight, but we can help improve your mental state. You need to get out of bed, Seh. You need to move around a lot more than you have been. Exercise will make you feel better."

"I can't walk without tripping over my own feet, Hok. I can't even stand without the world feeling like it's spinning. It's hopeless. Believe me, I've tried." Hok thought she heard his voice crack.

"I could help you learn to walk without tripping," Hok offered. "I know many different crane-style exercises to improve balance and dexterity, and most of them involve being blindfolded. The spinning sensation will go away with time. I felt dizzy for days when I started doing the exercises blindfolded, but I got used to it. Don't you remember seeing me doing them at Cangzhen?"

"Of course I remember," Seh replied. "I also remember you breaking a lot of things while you practiced."

"That happens," Hok said. "I've already talked to PawPaw about it. She doesn't mind."

"You're not going to leave me alone, are you?" Seh asked.

"No," Hok said. "In fact, beginning tomorrow I'll be near you more than ever. Cheen and Sum are leaving, and I'm going to move into this bedroom with you."

"Leaving?" Seh asked. "Where are they going?"

"Back to Kaifeng. You'll get a chance to say goodbye

to them in the morning. That is, if you get out of bed."

Seh pouted. "You're not going to give up, are you?"

"Never," Hok said. "So you may as well try some of the exercises."

Seh didn't reply.

"If you don't try," Hok joked, "I'll sit on my new bed here and stare at you all day and all night without blinking. You know I can do it. If you think me staring at you from the doorway was bad—"

"All right, all right." Seh sighed. "I'll give it a try. When do you want to start?"

Hok felt a smile creep up her face. "First thing tomorrow."

The next morning, Hok was surprised to wake to the sound of Seh's voice. She opened her eyes to find that he had gotten out of bed on his own and dressed in his gray peasant's robe and pants. He was at the far end of PawPaw's main room, talking with Cheen and Sum as they finished their packing. By the time Hok had wiped the sleep from her eyes and gotten out of bed, Cheen and Sum were ready to leave.

Hok helped Seh walk down to the river to say their final goodbyes. Seh held on to her arm the whole way, and he only slipped once on the slick yellow river mud near the water's edge. Hok thought it was a good start.

Hok was sorry to see Cheen and Sum go. However, she realized that Sum was completely healed and the two of them had to get on with their lives. Hopefully, she and Seh would do the same soon. After several long hugs and a few tears among themselves and PawPaw, Cheen and Sum shoved off aboard the battered old skiff that had brought them there. As soon as they were out of sight, Hok and Seh got to work.

Hok began Seh's training with an exercise that seemed simple enough but was surprisingly difficult. She had Seh stand on one leg. Hok knew firsthand that balancing on one foot with your eyes open is easy, but once your eyes are closed, everything changes. Grandmaster had made Hok practice standing on one leg blindfolded for hours on end, like a crane, when she was younger. Because of his own previous training, Seh had little trouble mastering this.

Hok decided to move on. She made Seh do one-legged squats next, with his raised leg held parallel to the ground. This Seh found more challenging, especially when Hok dared him to squat all the way down until his butt touched the ground. However, Seh quickly got the hang of this demanding exercise, too. Even better was the fact that Seh said his dizziness was beginning to subside.

Another nice side effect of the training was that Seh's snake seemed to be getting used to Hok being near it. When she would grab Seh now, if he lost his balance or needed a hand, the snake didn't appear to notice. Seh told her that snakes often grew accustomed to their handler's scent. While Hok wouldn't go so far as to touch the snake, she certainly felt less uneasy reaching out to Seh now.

Hok was feeling very good about Seh's rapid progress. She decided to keep pushing him.

Hok found an old board behind PawPaw's house and placed it over several small, flat rocks. The board formed a narrow walking platform that was twice as long as Seh was tall and rested only a few finger-widths off the ground. Hok held one of Seh's arms and made him walk across the board. This exercise was designed to both improve balance and teach a person to walk in a perfectly straight line. Hok knew how much this training had helped her, improving her skills to the point that she could easily walk blindfolded across a board spanning the distance between two Cangzhen rooftops. Fortunately, Seh didn't need to get to that level. By that evening, Hok was confident Seh had gotten all he needed out of this exercise.



After their evening meal, Seh said that he wanted to continue his training. PawPaw took over and showed Seh a few practical exercises that she had developed. Hok thought the most ingenious one was when PawPaw had Seh pour water and leave a single finger inside an empty cup so that he could feel how full it was.

Over the next three days, Hok taught Seh basic hand- and foot-juggling techniques. She used to practice these blindfolded, too, in order to help improve her reaction skills and timing. Hok thought that if Seh's hands and feet could react quickly enough to keep an object in the air, he could react fast enough to stationary objects while walking that he could avoid knocking them over. Seh had always had exceptionally fast hands thanks to his snake-style kung fu training, and he turned out to be an outstanding juggler.

On the fifth day, Hok had run out of things to teach Seh, so she took him into the forest and made him walk unassisted. Seh did remarkably well. Each time his foot met a rock or his outstretched hands touched a tree, he compensated and changed course in mid-stride, continuing forward without tripping or bumping into anything. He seemed to have developed a sixth sense almost overnight.

As strange as it sounded, Hok also thought that Seh's snake might be helping him in some way, too. On more than one occasion, Hok had seen the snake's head poke out of Seh's sleeve, tightening its body whenever Seh was dangerously close to bumping into something.

Whatever it was that led to Seh's new skills, the overall effect was that Seh's mood improved dramatically. He wasn't quite back to his old self, but he was definitely in much better spirits. PawPaw noticed, too. She took Hok aside at the end of the day.

"You've done well with Seh, Hok," PawPaw said. "You should be proud of yourself."

Hok shrugged. "I was only trying to help."

"Don't be so modest," PawPaw said. "You know you've done an excellent job. In fact, I'd venture to say that you've done all you can here."

Hok stared at PawPaw. "What are you saying?"

PawPaw smiled. "As much as I enjoy your company,

you and Seh should be getting on your way. It is time for you to spread your wings again."

Hok nodded slowly. "I was thinking the same thing. I'm going to miss you."

"I'll miss you, too," PawPaw said. "But you can always come back and visit. I'll welcome you with open arms, as will the villagers."

"That's right," Hok said. "The villagers. I'll have to make a point to go say goodbye to them."

PawPaw shook her head. "I wouldn't do that if I were you. The villagers will never forget what you've done, so a formal goodbye will serve no purpose other than to raise questions about where you are headed, and possibly where you've been. You were fortunate that they were too self-absorbed during their time of need to have questioned you. I don't think you should press your luck. Besides, it would add an air of mystery about you if you were to simply disappear after helping them."

"I understand," Hok said. "When do you think we should leave? In a couple of days?"

"Actually," PawPaw said, glancing at the evening sun, "I was thinking more like a couple of hours."

# CHAPTER 23

AnGangseh sat in the bow of the dragon boat, holding the stolen dragon scroll map up to the setting sun.

"Sssomething's not right," she said. "I sssuspect a sssnake in the grass."

Tonglong set his long push pole down and leaned toward his mother. "What do you mean?"

"Over the past month we've traveled the entire length of the Yellow River between Kaifeng and the Yellow Sssea," AnGangseh said. "We've explored every inlet, every outlet, and everything in between, yet we don't ssseem to be any closer to the treasure."

"Are you sure the map depicts the Yellow River?" Tonglong asked. "We're quite far north."

"Yesss," AnGangseh hissed. "I am sure. Your father

told me the details himself, right before he died. That was fifteen years ago, but I doubt the shorelines have changed drastically sssince. This dragon ssscroll map originated in the sssouth in our beloved Canton, but it is sssupposed to show the way to a treasure by ssstarting here in the north. The map does indeed include the Yellow River because many of the lines depicted match the shores we've ssseen. However, vast sssections appear disjointed." She rolled up the scroll and threw it to the floor of the boat. "I'm beginning to think sssomeone has tampered with it. If you look closely, in a few places it appears as though extra lines might have been sssketched in."

"What should we do?" Tonglong asked.

"We'll keep at it a few more days," AnGangseh said. "If we can't sssort it out, we'll hunt down those troublesome young monks and get to the bottom of this. I refuse to be made a fool of!"

# CHAPTER 24

Hok stood on the riverbank between PawPaw and Seh as the sun slowly dipped behind the western treetops upstream. Seh held on to Hok's right forearm, which she was thankful had completely healed. She had a feeling she would need both arms soon. On the shore beside her was a boat.

Hok glanced at it. It was a skiff similar to the one Cheen and Sum had left in, only smaller and in much better condition. This one was just big enough to carry two people, plus a few extra items. The skiff contained a large covered basket and a pile of what appeared to be clothes. Hok scratched her bald head and looked at PawPaw.

"Where did this boat come from?" Hok asked.

"It is my personal skiff," PawPaw said. "It's nearly as old as I am, but you can see that it is in fine condition. I dragged it out of its hiding place while you were working with Seh earlier today. It will serve you well."

Hok shook her head. "We can't take your boat, PawPaw. We'll walk."

"No, no," PawPaw said. "I haven't used this boat in years. I've been keeping it in working order for a time such as this. Besides, at this point you'd be doing me a favor. If you take it, I won't have to maintain it anymore. I'm getting too old for that kind of work."

Seh cleared his throat. "Couldn't we just walk? I'd like to put some of my new training to good use."

Hok half smiled and looked at PawPaw. "Seh doesn't like boats. Personally, I enjoy them, and I think a boat is the best method of transportation because I'd like to travel downstream. But I've never steered one before. Is it difficult?"

"Heavens, no," PawPaw said. "It's only tricky if you encounter rough water. However, I don't anticipate you'll find any. There will be plenty of easy, steady current. All you'll have to do is pole the skiff out to the center of the river and let it take you as far as you'd like to travel—all the way to the Yellow Sea, if you wish."

"That's it?" Hok asked.

"More or less," PawPaw said. "It's quite easy when the weather is calm like it is now. The skiff also has a small rudder at the rear that will allow you to steer. It's not that difficult to use. The main thing to remember is that when you push the rudder arm hard in one direction, it turns the boat in the opposite direction. That will take a little getting used to. Most of the time, you'll simply hold it in a fixed position. The farther you get downstream, the wider the river will be, which will make your job even easier because there is more room to navigate around obstacles. At some points, the river is more than half a *li* wide."

"What about other boats?" Hok asked.

"There aren't many other boats to worry about around here," PawPaw said. "Especially this late in the day. Jinan has a tremendous amount of boat traffic, but by the time you get there you should be accomplished enough to get by without too much trouble."



"Are you sure we shouldn't walk?" Seh asked. "Darkness is approaching after all, right?"

Hok watched PawPaw look up into the cloudless sky. "There will be plenty of moonlight to see by," PawPaw said. "It is better if you pass by the village at night. Someone might recognize my boat and chase you down. They might think you stole it."

"Are there many thieves around?" Hok asked. "I mean, should we keep an eye out for them?"

"There may be river pirates, I suppose," PawPaw said.

Hok's eyes widened. "River pirates?"

PawPaw nodded. "They are a rare breed in this region, but they are a threat nonetheless. You don't have anything of significant value, though, so even if you do bump into some, they shouldn't give you too much trouble."

"Are they tough?" Seh asked.

"They're not worth fighting, if that's what you're asking," PawPaw said. "It's best to give them what they want and be on your way. River pirates fight dirty, and they carry *qiangs.* I've heard rumors of a group that occasionally operates out of the Jinan City waterfront that is so ruthless, the local government is afraid to try and stop them and lets them have the run of the wharf. I have a feeling that that particular group won't bother you, though."

"What about the basket?" Hok said. "What's in it?"

"Just some provisions," PawPaw said. "There are also a couple of large hats to keep the sun off your heads. The river water reflects sunlight and magnifies it. You can burn very easily."

"Oh," Hok said. She didn't know what else she could say. PawPaw was too kind.

PawPaw walked past Hok, over to the side of the skiff. "Aren't you going to ask me about these, too?" PawPaw asked as she bent over and picked up the pile of clothes. Hok saw that it was a long, pale blue silk dress and an elegant matching turban. Beneath the clothes, still on the floor of the immaculate skiff, was PawPaw's straight razor.

PawPaw glanced first at the clothes, then at the razor. "Pick one," she said to Hok.

Hok understood. She was going to have to decide if she wanted to continue being a boy, or try being a girl again. Hok glanced down at her gray robes and ran her hand over her bald head. She found her decision surprisingly simple. She pointed to the dress and turban.

PawPaw smiled and handed the clothes to Hok. "A wise choice," she said, picking up the razor. "While you might be able to evade the Emperor's soldiers better as a boy, hiding your true self will take its toll over time. Embrace who you are and explore the new freedoms I'm sure it will bring. I suggest you keep the turban over your brown hair at all times, though. There's no need to be reckless. As far as we know, the Emperor's soldiers are still looking for you."

Hok nodded, then lowered her head. "I don't know how I'll ever be able to thank you."

"Stop that 'thank you' nonsense and go change," PawPaw said. "I want to see you in that dress!"

Hok ran up the hill to PawPaw's house. She put on the dress and turban, and ran back toward the riverbank with a huge smile on her face. The short-sleeve dress fit her better than she could have imagined. It covered her completely but still provided a full range of motion for her arms and legs. The cool silk felt wonderful against her skin, and she knew it looked nice against her pale features. It was perfect.

PawPaw's face brightened as Hok approached. "How lovely! You definitely made the right choice. You were born to be a girl!"

Hok blushed. She looked at Seh and saw that he was pouting. She wished Seh could see her now, too.

PawPaw snapped her fingers. "No pouting, Seh. This is a happy time. Where will the two of you be heading?"

Seh didn't answer.

Hok decided to answer for him. "We're not exactly sure. I thought traveling downstream made the most sense because there might still be soldiers upstream in Kaifeng looking for us. I haven't given it much more thought than that."

"I see," PawPaw said. "Can I make a suggestion?"

"Please," Hok said.

"If you don't mind, then," PawPaw said, "I'd like to take a peek at that map of yours, Seh. I overheard you talking with Hok about it last week, and I've been meaning to ask to see it ever since. I've spent my entire life in this region. Perhaps I can make some sense of it."

Hok was worried that Seh might decline, but he nodded and pulled the scroll from the small of his back. Hok saw his snake slither up his arm and over his shoulder.

"Here," Seh said, holding out the map.

PawPaw took it and unrolled it, holding the map up to the waning sunlight as she had undoubtedly heard Seh tell Hok to do. After a few moments, PawPaw whistled.

"Very, very clever," PawPaw said. "Look here, Hok. The main lines in the *chi* meridian sketch represent rivers, while the other lines represent tributaries and, possibly, landmarks. Pure genius."

"Is any of it familiar?" Hok asked.

"Yes," PawPaw said excitedly. "See this main meridian running across the chest of the figure from shoulder to shoulder? It represents the Yellow River. And see this main line that runs up and down the figure, from the head all the way to the feet? I believe it is the Grand Canal."

"What is the Grand Canal?" Seh asked.

PawPaw's eyebrows raised up. "You've never heard of the Grand Canal?"

Hok and Seh both shook their heads.

"Why, it is quite possibly the greatest engineering marvel of all time," PawPaw said. "It's a canal that extends from the capital city of Peking in the north, all the way to the city of Hangzhou in the south. It was dug entirely by hand. Most of China's rivers run west to east, so this canal is very, very important for north-south transportation of goods. If I had to guess, I'd say the head of this figure in your map represents the Emperor's palace in the Forbidden City inside Peking, which is the map's northernmost point. The feet represent something far to the south, but I'm not sure what. Perhaps Hangzhou, or some place even farther south like Canton. I've never traveled very far down the Grand Canal. I'm sorry I'm not much help."

"Don't be sorry," Hok said. "You've already been a really big help."

"Yes," Seh said. "We never would have figured that out. Or, at least I wouldn't have. Not in my condition."

PawPaw laid a hand on Seh's shoulder. "You're doing extraordinarily well, Seh. You should be happy with your progress. I don't want you to depart on a depressing note, okay?"

Seh nodded.

"Good," PawPaw said. "Do you happen to know what this map is supposed to lead to? A secret temple, perhaps?"

"We don't know," Hok replied. "But it seems to be very valuable. Seh is blind because—" Hok stopped herself in mid-sentence.

Seh cleared his throat. "It's okay, Hok. I'll tell her." He turned in PawPaw's general direction. "I was poisoned because AnGangseh wanted the original map. She stole it from me, but it won't do her any good. I changed it."

"You *what*?" Hok said. "You never told me you changed it!"

A crooked smile slithered up one side of Seh's face. "Sorry. I guess I forgot to mention it. I carefully drew several new lines that connected previously unconnected meridians on the original scroll. I also traced over all the other lines on the dragon scroll with new ink so that the ink would match everywhere."

"Dragon scroll?" PawPaw said. "You mean this is a copy of a dragon scroll map?"

Seh nodded. "Yes, why?"

"Well, this is only a legend, but it may be worth sharing," PawPaw said. "NgGung once told me a story about a secret dragon scroll map brought to Cangzhen by your Grandmaster. Supposedly, it leads to a treasure vault. NgGung thinks there might be some truth to it because your Grandmaster comes from a long line of bodyguards. His family has been protecting wealthy families for countless generations."

"You know," Seh said, "Grandmaster was constantly doing secret things and always seemed to have plenty of money. I wouldn't be surprised if he had a mountain of treasure hidden someplace."

"This certainly is exciting," PawPaw said. "Tell me, then, are the two of you going to head up the canal to the Forbidden City, or down into the southern regions?"

Hok paused, glancing at Seh. "We don't know," she said. "I'd like to try and find our brothers Fu and Malao before we go treasure hunting."

"Do you know where they've gone?" PawPaw asked.



"No," Hok replied. "They were abducted."

"Abducted?" PawPaw said, straightening up. "How come you never told me this?"

"I . . . I guess I didn't think there was anything you could do about it," Hok stammered. "I suppose I should have known better."

PawPaw took a deep breath and sighed. "No, you're probably right. There is no point in fretting about it now. There isn't much I could have done except tell NgGung to spread the word through his network to keep an eye out for them. I haven't seen NgGung since you've been here, though, so it doesn't matter. I'll be sure to tell him when I see him. Do you happen to know who took your brothers?"

“Fu was captured by a man called HaMo,” Hok said.

“I’ve heard the name,” PawPaw said. “He is not a nice man.”

Hok’s mind flashed back to the rainy day in the river. “I heard him say something to Fu,” she said to PawPaw. “HaMo said, ‘I like your spirit, boy. Forget your sister, I’m taking you to LaoShu instead.’ ” Hok sighed. “I don’t know what he meant by that, though.”

“I might,” PawPaw said. “Try not to think about what I said earlier concerning river pirates. I suggest you head to Jinan City—the City of Springs. It’s the next big city downriver, only a day’s travel from here. Seek out a place called the Jinan Fight Club.”

“What is that?” Hok asked.

“It’s exactly what it sounds like,” PawPaw said. “It’s a place where people fight and spectators gamble on the outcome. Many lives are foolishly lost for blood sport. It’s an evil place in the very heart of the city’s most elite section.”

“Is it difficult to find?” Hok asked.

“No,” PawPaw said. “But it’s difficult to get into. The crowd consists mostly of powerful officials. Jinan is the capital of the next province—Shandong. I wish there was something I could do to help you.”

Hok shook her head. “You’ve helped us so very much already.”

“That’s right,” Seh said. “We’ll never be able to thank you.”

PawPaw sighed. “Just take care of each other like you have been. That’s thanks enough for me. Now you two should be on your way." She looked up at the sky again. "You should be able to travel as long as you'd like by moonlight. If you can do without sleep, you can probably reach Jinan by sunrise. That might be best. The longer you're on the water during the day, the greater the chance that someone will see you and perhaps recognize you."

"I understand," Hok said.

"I do, too," Seh said.

"Then that is all," PawPaw said. She stepped between Hok and Seh and threw an arm around each of them, hugging them simultaneously. "I hope to see you both again someday."

"You will," Hok said, wiping her eyes. "I'll make sure of it."

"Me too," Seh added with a hint of a sniffle.



PawPaw wiped her own eyes, then helped Hok get Seh into the skiff. Hok and PawPaw pushed the skiff into the river, and Hok jumped aboard. She turned back to PawPaw and nodded once. PawPaw bowed back, then turned and headed up the hill toward her house.

Hok wiped her eyes again. She was going to miss PawPaw tremendously.

Hok grabbed the long push pole and quickly set a course down the center of the river. She missed her little brothers, too.

# CHAPTER 25

"Malao!" Fu said. "Can you hear me?"

Malao groaned and opened his eyes. "Huh . . . ?" he mumbled. "Where . . . where are we?"

"I don't know exactly," Fu replied.

"Is it . . . morning?" Malao asked. He glanced sleepily around the pitch-black room.

"I don't know," Fu said. "It's hard to tell without any windows."

"Ohhh," Malao said. "My whole body hurts. How long have I been asleep on this hard floor?"

"About a month," Fu replied.

"A month!" Malao said, sitting up. He bumped his head on a length of bamboo. "Ouch!" he yelled. "Hey—what . . . what's going on? Is this your idea of a joke?"

"I wish," Fu said. "We're in a cage. Don't you remember?"

"No," Malao said, rubbing his head. "All I remember is a bunch of crazy dreams. You wouldn't believe some of them. I dreamt about a cobra, a mantis, a toad, and a—" Malao stopped and stared in Fu's direction. "A tiger, too. I was *locked in a cage with it.*"

"I don't think those were dreams, Malao. You've been drugged."

"Drugged?"

Fu nodded in the darkness. "HaMo sprinkled a little bit of powder on your face every day. He called it Dream Dust."

"Yeah . . . ," Malao said wearily. "I had a dream about a river toad sprinkling dust beneath my nose. That was real?"

"Yes."

"I had a dream about a cobra choking me unconscious on a dragon boat in Kaifeng, too," Malao said. "Was that—"

"That was real, too," Fu said. "Hok, Seh, and I, plus Cheen and Sum from the bandit stronghold, tried to rescue you. We were ambushed by HaMo. Tonglong and AnGangseh showed up, too. That's how I got captured."

"Oh, no," Malao said. "I'm sorry."

Fu shrugged.

"Where are the others now?" Malao asked.

"I don't know."

"Hopefully, they're all right," Malao said.

"Yeah," Fu said. "Hopefully."

Malao yawned. "I can't believe how sleepy I am. Everything seems cloudy. Do you feel the same way?"

"No. HaMo tried to drug me at first, but I wouldn't let him near me. He tried to put some of that Dream Dust in my food, but I smelled it mixed in there. I refused to eat, and after a couple days he began to give me food without drugs."

"Whoa," Malao said. "You didn't eat for days? That's a first." He giggled weakly.

"This is serious, Malao. Although I'm glad you're awake, you should save the jokes for some other time."

Malao stopped giggling. "Sorry, Pussycat." He stretched and let out a long moan. "Everything seems to ache. If all I did was lay around asleep or drugged or whatever, why do I hurt so much?"

"Because you haven't moved around enough," Fu said. "Your muscles tighten up if you don't use them for a long time. HaMo pulled you out of your cage a few times to exercise your arms and legs, but that probably wasn't enough. Or maybe you're sore from what he did do. He bent and twisted you like a rag doll."

"I think I remember that," Malao said. "And I remember having my own cage. How did I end up in here with you?"

"HaMo put us in here a day and a half ago. Before that, we were locked in the same room, but kept in separate crates."

"Crates?" Malao said.

"They smelled like fruit," Fu said. "Apples, maybe. Whatever they were originally built for, they were too strong for me to break out of."

Malao scratched his head. "Are we in an orchard?"

"No, we're in a city called Jinan. HaMo nailed us inside the crates and shipped us here down the Yellow River along with a bunch of food."

Malao swallowed hard. "You don't think we're going to end up as . . . dumplings, do you, Pussycat?"

"I don't know. They've referred to us as 'fresh meat' several times. On the way to this room, we passed other rooms that had men in cages."

Malao shivered. "Who are 'they'? You don't mean that crazy old couple from the Divine Dumpling Inn?"

Fu shook his head. "I don't think so. When I say 'they,' I mean HaMo and his helpers."

Malao scratched his head again. "I wonder why they put us together."

"I think they have plans for us," Fu said. "Once they put you in here, they stopped drugging you. They probably want us to do something."

"Or maybe they're going to eat us!" Malao said. "They probably want to get all the drugs out of my system before they chop me up and . . ." His voice trailed off. "We need to get out of here, Fu."

"I know."

"So you've tried to escape?"

"A few times," Fu said. "Besides trying to break out

of the crates, I've tried to break out of this cage. But it's no use. This bamboo is too strong. I thought about putting up a fight when they first dumped you and me in here together, but several men with spears surrounded us the whole time and they had two ropes around my neck. I didn't have a chance. I—" Fu stopped in mid-sentence.

"What's wrong?"

"Shhh!" Fu whispered. "I hear footsteps."

"Over here, sir!" a muffled voice called out from outside the room. "You're just in time. It sounds like the small one has come out of his stupor, and they're discussing escape!"

"Escape?" a commanding voice replied. "We'll see about that."

Fu and Malao turned toward one another in the darkness. Someone had been listening to their every word. More than that, Fu and Malao both recognized the second person's voice!

A powerful teenager threw open the heavy door and stormed inside the dark room. His intense eyes reflected the dancing flames of the torch in his hands. "Well, well, well," he hissed at Malao and Fu. "How fortunate that you two should show up here at this time. We are expecting hundreds of guests soon, and they will be hungry for some fresh meat!"

Fu and Malao stared with their mouths agape.

The teen smirked and turned to the guard standing in the doorway. "Give me some time alone with these boys. I need to see what they are made of. A quarter of an hour should be sufficient. Make sure you lock the door behind you, too. If you hear screaming, pay it no mind. It will cease soon enough."

"I understand, sir," the guard replied with a wide grin. "Fresh meat always squeals the loudest." He laughed and bowed, then took a step back and closed the door.

# CHAPTER 26

Hok squinted downriver, staring into the rising sun. She and Seh had had an uneventful night. In fact, it had been downright boring. They hadn't encountered a single boat the whole time, and the traveling was easy. Hok was tired, but glad they'd stayed on the river without stopping. Jinan shouldn't be too far ahead.

Hok's stomach growled and her gaze drifted to the large basket PawPaw had placed in the skiff for them. They hadn't bothered to open it during the night.

"Are you hungry, Seh?" Hok asked.

Seh twitched, but didn't answer. He was asleep. Hok decided to leave him be.

Hok hooked one of the basket's large handles with

her foot and pulled it toward her. It was surprisingly heavy. She lifted the lid and found the two large hats PawPaw had mentioned, plus numerous containers of dried fruit and roasted nuts. There was enough food in there to last her and Seh at least a week.

Hok began to rummage through the items, taking care to keep the skiff on its steady course down the center of the river. At the very bottom of the basket, she noticed a corner of blue cloth. She grabbed hold of it and tugged. It was a large silk bag that matched her pale blue silk robe. Hok opened it and found an impressive collection of dried medicinal herbs. She grinned. PawPaw was the best.

Hok slipped the bag's single long strap around her neck and over one shoulder, then glanced over at Seh. He had curled into a ball on the floor of the skiff. Hok watched him sleep. The gentle rocking motion of the boat made keeping her eyes open a bit of a challenge, but she wanted to keep pressing onward. She also wanted to eat.

Hok looked up and saw a particularly narrow bend in the river ahead. Until now, the river had been growing increasingly wide, as PawPaw said it would. Hok sighed and replaced the lid on the basket. She would eat after she steered the boat through the bend and on to wider waters.

Hok glanced at the shore, then at the water, then back at the shore. She noticed that the current in this section of the river was pulling them along faster than previous sections. *Uh-oh,* she thought. With the fear of rapids creeping into her mind, Hok grabbed the rudder with both hands.

As she steered the boat into the curve, her grip tightened. Hok didn't see any rocks in the water, but there was an obstacle ahead that could prove to be far more dangerous. If the river had been a road, she would have been better prepared for the sight. However, being on the water, she had failed to recognize the bend for what it was—a natural choke point. The perfect place for an ambush.

Seh suddenly sat up, instantly awake. "Hok!" he whispered. "I sense something."

"Yes," Hok replied. "River pirates."

Hok scanned the river ahead of them and didn't like what she saw. Three sleek boats were anchored in a line across the width of the river. Each boat held four men wrapped head to toe in black cloth. The only thing visible was their eyes, which were staring in Hok's direction down *qiang* barrels.

"I sense a lot of negative energy," Seh said. "How many pirates are there?"

"Twelve," Hok replied, "and they all have *qiangs*."

"What do you think our chances are?" Seh asked.

"We don't have a chance," Hok said.

The pirate in the bow of the center boat waved his *qiang* and called out to Hok, "Steer toward me and prepare to be boarded!"

Hok lowered her voice to a whisper. "What should we do?"

"Do what they say," Seh replied. "Unless you have a better idea. Remember what PawPaw said about them."

Hok frowned. She was out of ideas. They were going to be boarded.

The center pirate boat was anchored with its bow facing upstream, and Hok pointed the bow of PawPaw's skiff at it. She let the strong current carry them downstream. The pirate boat was coming up fast.

"Slow down," the pirate leader called out.

*Slow down?* Hok thought. *How am I supposed to do that?*

The pirate leader raised his *qiang*. "Slow your vessel down immediately."

"I don't know how!" Hok said.



"Do you expect me to fall for that?" the pirate leader said. "Slow down and turn to port."

"I have no idea what 'port' is," Hok shouted back. They were getting dangerously close to the pirate leader's boat. "Help me!"

"Port is left!" the pirate said. "Turn to port now, young lady! Men, cut the lines and heave us to port, too! We're in opposition. We'll swing around each other."

"Hang on, Seh!" Hok cried, and she shoved the rudder with all her might to the left. The skiff made a sharp turn—to the right. She had forgotten that the rudder steered the boat in the opposite direction. They were going to collide! Hok slammed her eyes shut.

*THUMP!*

"Arrgh!" the pirate leader shouted as his vessel rocked violently sideways. Hok opened her eyes and watched the bow of PawPaw's skiff scrape along the side of the pirates' boat. Hok avoided eye contact with the scrambling pirates, who were close enough to touch.

Hok felt PawPaw's skiff begin to slip away from the pirates' boat, and she straightened the rudder. The skiff began to nose its way downriver again with Seh at the bow, gripping the sides like his life depended on it.

"After them!" the pirate leader shouted. "Perimeter sailors, take aim! Vessel One, fire at will!"

*BANG! BANG! BANG! BANG!*

Four shots rang out. Hok heard two *qiang* balls slam into the bow of the skiff a hand's-width from Seh.

"No!" Hok cried. She looked back at the pirate leader's advancing boat. The three men with him were paddling frantically, trying to catch up with her and Seh. She heard the pirates shouting to one another in a different language.

"Vessel One, reload!" the pirate leader commanded.

"Stop it!" Hok shouted. "Please! I didn't mean to ram into you! It was an accident!" The pirate leader's boat was gaining on them. Hok looked at the pirate leader's masked face, and they locked eyes. Hok nearly tumbled out of the boat. His eyes were round and blue as the sky, just like Charles'.

"Vessel Two, prepare to fire on my command!" the pirate leader roared.

"No!" Hok said. "Why are you doing this?" She heard more shouting in another language.

"On my mark!" the pirate leader shouted.

"NO!" Hok screamed. She had to think of something. She heard more foreign language shouting and saw several pirates point toward the sky. A shadow passed overhead and Hok looked up to see a large crane flying straight toward the pirates that were taking aim with their loaded *qiangs.* The bird appeared frightened, probably startled by the *qiangs* that had just been fired. A black-and-white sticky goo began to pour from beneath its tail feathers, and several pirates shouted angrily as their heads and shoulders were splattered with globs of the foul stuff. One of the men yelled a string of words that Hok didn't understand, finishing with the word *crane.*

Hok could hardly believe her ears. She realized the pirate hadn't said the word *crane* in Mandarin or even Cantonese. He had said it in Dutch.

Something clicked inside Hok's head, and many of the words the men were shouting to one another began to make sense. The pirates spoke her father's language!

"Take aim!" the pirate leader bellowed, raising one arm high.

"NEE!" Hok shouted at the top of her lungs. "NEE! NEE! NEE! NO! NO! NO!"

The pirate leader's body went rigid, and pirate

mouths across the river dropped. Hok stared at the pirate leader, desperation on her face.

The pirate leader lowered his arm and spoke to Hok in Chinese. "What did you just say?"

Hok answered in Dutch. "I said, *no*?"

The pirate leader's eyes narrowed. "Pull alongside them, men!" he ordered, and the men in his boat eased their vessel alongside PawPaw's skiff.

Hok watched Seh release his grip on the skiff and form snake-head fists with both hands. He sat perfectly still, his snake writhing beneath his sleeve.

The pirate leader stared hard at Hok, and he spoke in Dutch. "So, you understand me, girl?"

"Yes . . . ," Hok replied, struggling to remember words she hadn't used in more than nine years. "I . . . understand some. Chinese is better for me, though, if you please."

The pirate leader switched back to Chinese. "Why didn't you say something when the men were shouting among themselves in Dutch?"

"I don't know," Hok replied. "It all happened so fast. I didn't realize they were speaking Dutch until the crane flew overhead. I have not used the language in many years."

"Who taught you to speak it?" the pirate leader asked.

"My father."

"What is his name and occupation?"

"His name is Henrik," Hok said. "He is the captain of a trading ship."

The pirate leader's eyebrows went up. He glanced around at his men. "Lower your *qiangs*!" he shouted. To Hok he said, "Remove your turban."

Hok did as she was told. She felt the warmth of the rising sun wash over the brown stubble on her head.

The pirate leader nodded. He turned to the perimeter boats and made an announcement. "Crewmen of Vessel One, you will remain anchored here with all hands aboard. For you, it's business as usual. Crewmen of Vessel Two, go clean the bird droppings off yourselves and the boat and get back here on the double." He looked at the men in his boat. "You three are coming with me. It appears we have a special delivery to make."

"Aye, sir!" the men in all three boats responded.

The pirate leader turned to Hok. "Do you think you can follow us in your skiff—without the ramming this time?"

Hok felt her face begin to blush. "I can try."

"Come on, then," the pirate leader said. "I know someone who would very much like to see you."

# CHAPTER 27

Two hours later, Hok found herself navigating awkwardly between an unbelievable number of boats. Everything from large seafaring junks to tiny one-person vessels bumped and banged against one another as they vied for limited dock space at the Jinan wharf.

Hok followed as close behind the pirate leader as she dared, trying not to ram him. She was both relieved and a little concerned when she saw him begin to steer toward an empty dock guarded by several large foreign men. It appeared to be a private dock with no other boats around, so docking there would be relatively easy. On the other hand, the foreigners guarding it all carried *qiangs* and every man was staring at her and Seh, pointing and talking. One of the men ran off the dock, onto the shore, and disappeared up a crowded street that ran parallel to the wharf.

The pirate leader eased his boat up to the far side of the dock and climbed up a short ladder while his men secured the vessel. He stepped onto the dock and motioned for Hok to tie up on the opposite side. As Hok neared, the pirate leader gave her simple directions to help her approach the dock broadside. It was difficult work for her, not only because she didn't know what she was doing but also because she was anxious. She couldn't stop thinking about what the pirate leader had said earlier about someone who would like to see her.

PawPaw's skiff bumped against one of the dock's massive support piers, and the pirate leader began to secure the skiff to the dock with several ropes. Her work complete, Hok gazed up at the pirate leader's face. He had removed his mask more than an hour ago, but this was the first time she had a chance to get a good look at him. She was surprised to see that he had a strong, very kind face.

When the pirate leader finished, he helped Hok climb onto the dock. Hok, in turn, leaned over the skiff to help Seh. The pirate leader shot her a quizzical look.

"He's blind," Hok said. She glanced at Seh and saw his jaw tighten.

"You don't say?" the pirate leader said. "I would

never have guessed. He appears so . . . comfortable. I'll help him out."

The pirate leader leaned in front of Hok and reached for Seh's arm, but Seh jerked away. At the same time, Seh's snake poked its head out of his sleeve and hissed at the pirate.

The pirate leader jumped back. "What the devil?"

"I'll get out myself, thanks," Seh said.

Hok watched the pirate leader's expression as Seh quickly climbed onto the dock unassisted and stood. The man was clearly impressed.

Seh's snake pulled its head back beneath his robe, and Seh glanced in Hok's direction. "Ready to go ashore?" he asked. "I am."

"Just a moment," Hok said. She got down on her hands and knees and reached into the skiff, grabbing her turban. She also removed the lid from the basket and took out one of the large floppy hats, plus a container of dried fruit. Hok replaced the lid and stood.

"Here," Hok said, placing the hat over Seh's thick black hair. "It will help hide your identity, just in case."

"It's better to be safe than sorry," Seh said, pulling the rim down low over his eyes.

"Good thinking," the pirate leader said.

Hok tied the turban back over her brown stubble and ran her eyes over PawPaw's skiff.

"It's a lovely craft, isn't it?" the pirate leader said. "Old, yet strong, as your ramming proved. My men will keep an eye on it for you, as well as your basket."

"Thank you," Hok said. She stretched and looked around, scanning the surrounding docks closely for the first time. There were many more large junks than she would have expected. They were still quite some distance from the sea. The boats were either being loaded or unloaded with untold quantities of merchandise. It was a trader's paradise. However, Hok's gaze didn't stay long on the junks with their large, fixed sails reinforced with bamboo. She was looking for her father's foreign-designed ship with its numerous masts and multiple billowing sails. Unfortunately, she couldn't match the image of the ship she had in her head with any of the vessels here.

"Are you all right, Hok?" Seh asked. "I sense that you are tense."

"I'm just a little nervous," Hok replied. "I haven't seen my father since I was three years old."

"Your father?" the pirate leader said. "What makes you think he's here?"

Hok's face flushed. "You mean he's not here?"

"No. He's away."

"But I thought you said—"

"I said that I know someone who would like very much to see you," the pirate leader interrupted. "I never said that it was your father."

"This had better not be some kind of cruel joke," Seh hissed. "Do you even know her father?"

The pirate leader laughed. "Do I know her father? I am his first mate!"

Hok stared at the man. "But that would mean that my father is a . . ."

"Pirate?" the pirate leader offered.

"Yes," Hok said. "That can't be true."

"No?" the pirate leader asked. He pointed toward shore, up the crowded street. "Why don't you ask *him*? He's the person I was referring to."

A familiar voice called out to Hok in heavily accented Chinese. She looked over and saw a pale teenager running toward them with something in one hand.

"Is that Charles?" Seh asked.

"Yes," Hok replied.

The pirate leader cleared his throat. "I can see that the three of you have *a lot* of catching up to do. I'll be leaving now. Nice meeting you both." He nodded and walked to shore, heading up the street with two of the dock guards in tow. He nodded to Charles as they passed each other, and Charles nodded back.

Hok put her face in her hands. "I can't believe this, Seh. My father is a pirate captain."

"Well, if it makes you feel any better," Seh replied, "your father can't be any worse than my mother."

Hok shook her head. She wasn't sure if she wanted to laugh or cry.

"Here comes Charles," Seh said.

Hok lifted her head and saw Charles approaching. She could feel his heavy footfalls on the dock. Seh had obviously felt them, too.

Charles stopped in front of Hok and stood there,

sucking wind. Once he had caught his breath, he said, "I'm so glad you're here."

Hok frowned. "I'm glad to see you, too, I suppose."

Charles' brow wrinkled. "You don't sound very glad. What's wrong?"

"You're a pirate, Charles," Hok said. "How come you never told me?"

"I . . . I don't know," Charles replied. "I guess I thought you knew."

"Well, I didn't know," Hok said. "My mother told me that you and Father worked for the Resistance. She said you transport things."

"We do," Charles said. "We transport *qiangs*. You at least knew that much, right?"

"So what if I did?" Hok asked.



"Where do you think the *qiangs* come from?"

"I have no idea."

"They come from shipments we intercept along the Yellow River," Charles said. "Shipments bound for the Emperor's troops. We take *qiangs* that would normally be used to kill innocent villagers and warrior monks and—"

"What do *you* use the *qiangs* for?" Hok interrupted in an icy tone.

"Nothing yet," Charles replied.

"Nothing?" Hok said. She pointed to the two holes the pirates had shot in the bow of PawPaw's skiff. "You call *that* nothing?"

Charles looked at the *qiang* holes and his pale face grew even whiter. "I am so sorry, Hok. I had no idea."

"Of course you didn't," Hok said. "Just don't tell me that you and your pirate friends are doing 'nothing' with the *qiangs* you steal. I know better."

"Hey!" Charles said. "I'm trying to apologize. Sometimes people make mistakes. Our men usually only fire upon people who attack them first." He glanced again at the bow of PawPaw's skiff. "How did your boat get so banged up in the front?"

"We had an accident," Seh replied.

"I see," said Charles. He turned to Hok. "For your information, the bandits use our *qiangs,* too. I can't understand why you have a problem with pirates but don't seem to have a problem with bandits. We basically do the same thing. Your father can explain it better than I can. He's away on business but should return soon."

Hok stared hard at Charles, frustrated. She wanted to know more, but she didn't want to ask.

Charles glanced at the armed men on the dock and sighed. He leaned toward Hok and lowered his voice. "We keep a few *qiangs* for our own uses, obviously, but we give the vast majority of them to Resistance members in several different regions. They are stockpiling them."

Seh stepped closer to Hok and took her arm. "Why do you care so much about this Resistance, Charles?" he asked.

"Yes, Charles," Hok said. "Why do you care?"

Charles looked suddenly hurt. "I care because your father cares, Hok. He's done more for me than you can ever imagine. And before you even ask, *he* cares because your mother cares. So, if you have any more questions about that, you should talk to Bing. Right now, I'm just trying to help *you*."

Hok frowned.

"I'm trying to help your brothers, too," Charles said. "What do you think I'm doing here in Jinan? Look." He held out his hand.

Hok saw that the object he had been holding was a piece of rolled-up parchment.

"These postings are hanging on all of the Jinan message boards," Charles said. "Your father's men saw them and sent word to your mother and me. I decided to come here and see if I could do anything to help."

Charles unrolled the document and Hok's eyes widened.



"What does it say?" Seh asked.

Charles glanced suspiciously at Seh. "Can't you read it?"

"Seh is having some trouble with his eyes right now," Hok said.

"Oh," Charles replied. "I'm sorry. Are you going to be all right, Seh?"

"I'll be fine," Seh said. "Just read the posting, please."

Hok cleared her throat.

## FRESH MEAT TONIGHT!

ATTENTION, ONE AND ALL:

TWO VICIOUS YOUNG ENEMIES OF THE STATE HAVE BEEN CAPTURED.

Now by special arrangement with the Emperor's High Court, the convicts will receive their punishment during the regularly scheduled fights at my spectacular entertainment venue—the Jinan Fight Club. All your favorites will be there! The fights are sure to be brutal! Death is a strong possibility! Don't miss the action!

Open to the public.
Your Gracious Host and
Fight Promoter,
LaoShu

"Fu and Malao?" Seh asked.

"Yes," Hok said. "There is a sketch of both of them."

"It sounds serious," Seh said.

"It is," Charles replied. "LaoShu is an evil man."

"Then we'd better start planning something immediately," Seh said.

"I agree," Hok said. "But there's something else you need to know first. There is a third sketch, Seh." She pointed to the poster. "Charles, do you know who this is?"

"Sure," Charles replied. "Everyone in Jinan knows who he is. That's the Golden Dragon, the current Jinan Fight Club champion. He's a real crowd pleaser. Why do you ask?"

"We know him, too," Hok said. "He's our brother Long."

# CHAPTER 28

Malao and Fu sat next to one another, staring out through the bars of the bamboo cage. Before them in the center of the dark room stood their thirteen-year-old brother Long, holding a torch. He wore a green silk robe and red silk pants, bound by a red sash—the uniform of the new Emperor. Long's taut, powerful muscles flexed beneath the fine silk.

Malao grinned weakly. "That guard just called me 'fresh meat.' He obviously doesn't know me very well." Malao lifted one of his smelly feet into the air and wiggled his dirty toes. "This certainly isn't fresh!" He began to giggle.

"No laughing, prisoner!" Long snarled. While his voice was harsh, he winked in a playful manner and pointed the torch back toward the closed door.

Inside the cage, Fu leaned over and whispered forcefully into Malao's ear, "Don't you remember that that guard overheard every word we said earlier *through* the door? Keep your voice down!"

Malao lowered his foot.

Long crossed the room and knelt in front of Fu and Malao's cage. "Are you two all right?" he asked in a whisper.

Fu lowered his voice to a deep rumble. "I am fine, but Malao's head is cloudy. He was drugged for more than a month. He just woke up."

"Drugging newcomers is common here," Long said. He looked at Malao. "You'll have a few rough nights, but after that you'll be back to your old self. You'll have to sweat the drugs out of your system."

Malao nodded. "What is this place?"

"It's a prison," Long said. "Or at least the lower half is. The upper section is a huge dining hall with an enormous pit in the center. The pit extends all the way down to this level. You'll see it soon, unfortunately."

"What do you mean by 'unfortunately'?" Fu asked. "What is the pit used for?"

"Fighting," Long replied. "People come from far and wide to watch the fights and place bets. It's brutal. The prisoners fight locals, often to the death."

Malao swallowed hard. "The rich people don't eat the . . . uh . . . losers, do they?"

"Of course not," Long said. "What ever gave you an idea like that?"

"Don't ask," Fu replied. "Why did that guard call us 'fresh meat'?"

"It's the term used for first-time fighters," Long said. "They are often served up as an easy match for top-level fighters."

"So we're going to have to fight?" Malao asked.

"I'm afraid so," Long said. "I won't be able to help you escape. This place is too secure. If you win enough fights, however, you'll be set free and any charges against you will be forgiven. You two were brought here as Enemies of the State, which is a common charge. You could be out in a year, as long as you keep winning."

"A year!" Malao said.

"Shhh!" Long whispered. "I'll do what I can to help you, but my hands are tied. Like I said, this place is too secure."

"What are *you* doing here?" Fu asked.

"I heard about the fight club from one of Grandmaster's visitors," Long said. "I came straight here after the attack and convinced the fight promoter, a man called LaoShu—*Rat*—that I was a local. He has no idea about my history at Cangzhen, and I need to keep it that way."

"You came here on purpose?" Malao said. "Why?"

"Prisoners fight for their freedom," Long said. "But locals fight to join the Emperor's ranks. There are fight clubs like this one in several regions, and each year the champions from each club meet to fight each other. The winner is awarded a military post. That's how Ying became a major under the Emperor so quickly and at such a young age. He was last year's Grand Champion. I hope to do the same thing."

Fu scratched his head. "Why?"

"Grandmaster told us to change Ying and to change the Emperor's heart," Long said. "I decided that the best way to do that was from the inside. It hasn't been easy, but so far it's working. I'm currently the top fighter here, which is why I'm wearing this uniform and why I have access to you. It's my job to determine the skill level of each new prisoner. LaoShu organizes the fights, and like a rat he is very clever. He already knows about your background, and he has placed both of you in the elite category."

"So, if you're not going to evaluate us, why are you with us now?" Malao asked.

Fu growled. "He came to tell us that we're going to fight soon, right?"

"Yes," Long said. "That's why they stopped drugging Malao. They want him to have a relatively clear head."

"Great," Malao said. "Some guy that never met me is going to try to beat me to a pulp so that he can be a soldier." He rubbed his temples. "My head is still so foggy. This isn't fair. Why were we captured and brought to this prison fight club thing in the first place? Was there a reward or something?"

"Yes, there is a price on all our heads," Long said. "Ying saw to that. I've been lucky that no one has identified me. There is a special price for Hok because of an attack that occurred against Shaolin Temple. You haven't seen her, have you?"

"She was with us for a little while," Fu said. "So was Seh. We're not sure what happened to them after we were captured, though."

"I see," Long said. "Let's hope that they are all right. If they do get caught, I expect they'll end up here."

"For the reward?" Fu asked.

"That, and the gambling element," Long replied. "The man who brought you here, HaMo, believes you can both fight well. Most people will bet against you because you're young, but HaMo has already placed large bets in your favor. I've heard rumors that he's bet all of the reward money he collected for your captures. If you both win, he will be a very rich man."

Malao stared at Long in the flickering torchlight. "Do you think we will win?"

"I'm not going to lie," Long said. "The competition here is very tough. These fighters use a combination of simple but effective techniques from a wide variety of styles, and everyone cheats. There are no rules. Grappling is popular, so practice your mount escapes while you have time. Watch out for armlocks and leglocks."

"Who are we fighting?" Fu asked.

"That hasn't been determined yet," Long said. "You won't know until they lead you into the pit. Now, I suggest you start practicing. Don't wear yourselves out, though. Go easy."

"Go easy?" Malao said, rubbing his head. "When are we fighting?"

Long frowned. "Tonight."

# CHAPTER 29

"Look at this," AnGangseh said, pointing to a posting on the Jinan wharf bulletin board. "You were right. HaMo brought the boys here."

"It says the fights are tonight," Tonglong said, scanning the announcement. "It's already getting dark. We had better hurry."

"Do you remember how to get there?" AnGangseh asked.

"Of course," Tonglong said. "It's only been two years since I won the Grand Championship here."

AnGangseh grinned. "Your performance that night was unforgettable. Perhaps you can use sssome of those sssame techniques on your brother, Ssseh?"

"We'll see if he's here," Tonglong said. "He may not have survived the river."

"He sssurvived," AnGangseh said. "The girl went after him. She is ssstrong, I can tell. She is sssmart, too—and lucky. I have a feeling they will both be at the fight club."

Tonglong tugged on the tiny green crane around his neck. "Perhaps we should have finished off her and Seh when we had the chance."

"What's past is past," AnGangseh said. "Don't give it a sssecond thought. If she is at the fight club, you will get your chance. That is, unless I get my hands on her first. Let's go. I have had enough of these children from Cangzhen."

# CHAPTER 30

It took Hok, Seh, and Charles until early evening to get to the Jinan Fight Club. The distance wasn't too great, but the city was incredibly crowded—even more so than Kaifeng. Hok had never seen so many people.

The going was also slower with Seh on Hok's arm. Seh did a superb job of staying on his feet, but every step they took took longer than it would have if Seh had been his old self. Hok tried not to think about it, but she decided that Seh had been right. His mother had to be worse than her father ever could be.

Once they finally got into the fight club line, it was another three hours before they reached the front door. It seemed the men guarding the entrance were very particular about who they let in, and they took their time making their decisions. Hok saw far more people turned away than let in.

Hok adjusted the elegant turban on her head and straightened her dress, shifting her bag full of herbs directly in front of her so that she could keep a close eye on it once they got inside. Charles had guaranteed that they wouldn't be turned away. She hoped he was right.

Hok glanced down at Seh's bulging midsection. He had several lengths of rope wrapped around his waist beneath his gray robe that served to both disguise his physique and, hopefully, aid in their rescue attempt. Seh's snake was a barely noticeable lump coiled around his left forearm, beneath his sleeve. Hok looked at the large hat Seh still wore pulled low across his brow and doubted either she or Seh would be recognized in their headwear, which made them both look much older than twelve. Still, she hoped age wasn't a consideration for entry here.

It turned out age wasn't an issue for them getting in, nor was anything else. Charles had Seh's coin pouch tied to his own sash, and he handed the guard at the door ten times the normal entry fee. They were allowed inside without any questions. Charles then handed more money to a seating attendant.

The three of them were led deep into the crowded fight club, down a series of tiered sections that sank lower and lower toward a large circular hole in the center of the room. Seh took Hok's arm and remained glued there, doing an admirable job of weaving around tables, chairs, and, most of all, groups of people dressed in fine silk robes and fancy hats. Fortunately, some crowd members wore simple gray peasant's robes like Seh was wearing. They all fit in just fine.

As they walked, Hok noticed that Charles hadn't uttered a single word. He had told her earlier that "money talks" in Jinan and that foreign merchants often try to earn trading rights with local businessmen by treating them to extravagant nights at the fight club. Charles had also said that they would be sure to see several tables of Chinese men accompanied by one or two "round eyes," usually a foreign ship captain plus his cabin boy or servant. Hok did see several examples of this throughout the room, and she knew that it would work to their advantage. Charles could sit with them without raising any eyebrows.

Their final destination was a choice table on the very edge of the fighting pit. Charles nodded to the attendant as if pleased, and handed over even more money. The attendant nodded back, and left.

Hok found herself at the heart of the Jinan Fight Club. She quickly scanned the room. Small wooden tables draped in blood-red silk ringed the enormous round fighting pit, with larger silk-covered tables radiating outward and upward on the tiered wooden floor all the way to the building's tapestry-covered walls. An oil lamp sat on every table, giving the entire room an orange glow. Torches protruding from the pit's inner walls added additional light to the fighting area, as well as a fair amount of black smoke.

Hok noticed that the lamps on several tables were not burning. The effect left the people sitting at those tables in relative obscurity. She liked that. Hok blew out the oil lamp on their table and helped Seh sit down. Charles excused himself to get something for them to eat from a nearby vendor, and Hok took a seat next to Seh.

Hok folded her arms, resting them on a thick metal railing that surrounded the fighting pit, and looked down into the pit for the first time. It was enormous, as deep as four men were tall, and formed a perfect circle. Hok guessed it was at least fifty paces across. The sides and bottom were covered with rough bricks, and there was a large door at one end. The door was closed.

"What does the pit look like?" Seh asked.

"It's deep," Hok replied.

Seh tapped his bulging midsection and lowered his voice. "Do you think the rope is long enough? It wraps around my waist seven times."

"The rope definitely won't reach the bottom of the pit," Hok replied, "but it still might work. Fu and Malao can jump and probably reach it. That is, if we even get a chance to throw it to them."

"We've come this far," Seh said. "We need to at least try and help them escape."

"I agree," Hok said.

Charles returned carrying three small drinking bowls of fruit juice and three bundles of sticky rice wrapped in lotus leaves, all on a tray. He set the tray on the table and plopped down in his chair, handing the pouch of coins to Seh. "I can't believe I just spent the equivalent of two years' wages."

"You did use a lot of coins," Seh said, weighing the bag in his hand. "Thanks. It's very difficult for me, not being able to see."

"No problem," Charles said. "It made more sense for me to handle everything anyway, with the color of my skin and all. It's supposed to look like I'm treating you." He paused. "If you don't mind my asking, where did you get all that money?"

"From my father," Seh replied, tying the pouch to his sash. "Is there much left?"

"No," Charles said. "But I was thinking, you could bet some of it on Fu and Malao. If the odds are good and they win, you could get all your money back, and more."

"That's a good idea," Seh said, "but I don't plan to stick around long enough to collect the winnings. I'll just hang on to what we have. The funny thing is, this money is winnings from a different fight Malao was in."

Charles' eyebrows raised. "Really? I never heard this story."

"Another time," Seh said. "We should keep our talking to a minimum."

"Right," Charles said. He looked over toward the

back corner of the fight club, and Hok followed his gaze. There were a large number of people crowded around a small table.

"I think I'll go take a look at the bettors' table," Charles said. "Maybe I can find out when Fu and Malao are fighting."

"Good idea," Hok replied.

Charles stood and Hok watched him walk over to the cluster of people who were exchanging strings of coins for bamboo sticks with writing on them. As Charles began to muscle his way into the group, a door opened off to one side of the bettors' table. Out walked HaMo with a fistful of wager sticks. Behind him was a tall, thin man with a large pointy nose, short greasy hair, and tiny, perky ears. There was no doubt this man was LaoShu—*Rat*.



Behind LaoShu came ten soldiers with *qiangs*, surrounding an additional person. Hok couldn't see who it was, but he—or she—was obviously very important. Hok also couldn't help but notice a soldier in the group who stood at least three heads taller than everyone else in the room. Hok had seen extraordinarily large men before, including Hung and Mong, but this soldier dwarfed them all. She could hardly believe he was human. He had wide, thick shoulders, long black hair, and an expressionless gaze as cold as stone.

People in the crowd began to notice LaoShu and the soldiers, and the fight club fell silent. The cluster of bettors even quieted down.

HaMo separated from the group and sat alone at a

small table in back with his back to the wall. LaoShu and the soldiers walked down several tiers toward a long empty table at the edge of the pit, opposite Hok and Seh. As the group slowly descended, people began to whisper excitedly.

Hok watched the group, and they soon descended to a point where Hok could catch a glimpse of the important person. It was a man, and he was wearing a brilliant yellow robe as bright as the sun. Only one person in all of China was allowed to wear a yellow robe—the Emperor.

A small drum sounded, and all eyes turned anxiously to LaoShu, who had reached the edge of the pit. The Emperor sat down, and the enormous man took the seat to the Emperor's right. A different soldier sat down in the chair to the Emperor's left, and Hok's heart skipped a beat. She recognized the man's bald head and bushy eyebrows. It was General Tsung.

"Seh!" Hok whispered. "General Tsung is here! So is the Emperor! They're sitting directly across the pit from us."

Seh frowned. "I'll be sure to keep my head down."

"Me too," Hok said, pulling her turban low on her forehead. "I wonder who else will show up."

"I don't even want to think about it," Seh replied.

Charles rushed back over to their table and sat down. "LaoShu is about to make the opening announcements," he said.

LaoShu cleared his throat and began to speak loudly in a squeaky, high-pitched voice.

"Welcome, everyone, to my world-famous Jinan Fight Club! I hope you're enjoying our hospitality. Tonight we have what may be our most impressive lineup ever, both inside the pit and out. I'd like to begin by welcoming the most distinguished guest to ever grace this humble establishment. Ladies and gentlemen, pay your respects to our beloved Emperor! *Kowtow!*"

The crowd members, including LaoShu, dropped to their knees.

"Seh, kneel," Hok whispered, and she helped Seh to the floor. They both knocked their foreheads against the ground three times, as did Charles. Their respects complete, Hok helped Seh back into his chair, and she sat down between Seh and Charles.



In front of the pit, LaoShu stood and continued the announcements.

"It is both an honor and a pleasure for me to announce two additional guests, neither of whom is a stranger to this arena. First is a man who achieved special notoriety within the Emperor's ranks in an impressively short period of time. Everyone, show your appreciation for the Fight Club Grand Champion of China from several years ago—General Tsung, the Leopard Monk!"

Applause erupted from the audience, and Tsung stood and bowed. Several people from the crowd pointed at him and waved. Others pointed toward the giant sitting to the Emperor's right.

"I see several of you have already spotted our third

distinguished guest," LaoShu announced. "He really stands out in a crowd, if you know what I mean! He's another former Grand Champion, who also happens to be the Emperor's chief security officer and personal bodyguard. Ladies and gentlemen, the most dangerous man to ever grace our pit—Xie, the Scorpion!"

The crowd's cheering was even louder and more frenzied for Xie, and Seh leaned over in Hok's general direction. "What does this Scorpion look like?" he asked.

"Trouble," Hok replied.

The crowd began to quiet down, and LaoShu clapped his hands. "I told you tonight was going to be special! Now, just listen to what will be happening *inside* the pit. Not one, but *two* Enemies of the State will face the consequences for their treasonous actions before your very eyes. We also have a handful of lesser criminals, all of whom have promised they'll not go down without a fight. As for your local heroes, you'll see many of your favorites tonight, including the top contender to represent Jinan in the upcoming championships—the young wonder who calls himself the Golden Dragon. What do you think about that!"

The crowd began to cheer and yell and stomp their feet. Hok watched a huge toothy smile spread across LaoShu's face.

"I hope you've placed your wagers," LaoShu announced, "because betting on this first bout is about to close. Wagering odds for the upcoming bouts can be found at the bettors' table. As always, once the gong sounds, the action will officially begin and all betting on that bout will cease. And now, it is with great excitement that I bring you the first bout of the evening! It will feature two hardened criminals making their inaugural appearances here on the road to possible freedom. First into the pit is a powerhouse from the northernmost regions. He needs little introduction from me. His physique speaks for itself! Ladies and gentlemen, let's hear some applause for the Mongolian Mauler!"

The large door inside the pit flew open and Hok watched a tall, thick-muscled man with short black hair walk proudly into the pit wearing only a heavy loincloth. The crowd clapped its approval.



LaoShu continued. "The challenger hails from a foreign land known as Siam. He's a small man with a big heart. Don't let his size fool you. His techniques are as exotic as his language. Everyone, get ready for the Siamese Assassin!"

Hok saw a thin, wiry young man dance into the pit through the open doorway. His hair was also short, but unlike the Mauler, his skin was quite dark and he wore short pants that stopped above his knees. The rest of his skin was bare except for a narrow decorative band tied around the upper part of each of his biceps.

Hok stared at the young man's hands. Curiously, they were wrapped with rope. The rope looked very rough and covered everything but his fingers, which moved freely. Hok assumed it would allow him to both grab things and make fists.

Hok leaned toward Seh. "Do you want me to tell you what I see?"

"Don't bother," Seh replied. "Just tell me who is going to win."

"The Siamese Assassin," Hok said.

"What?" Charles said. "Are you crazy? The other man is huge!"

Hok shook her head. "That doesn't matter."

"Huh?" Charles said. "What *does* matter?"

"See the shiny line running down each of the Assassin's shins?" Hok said. "All the hair has been worn off his legs in those spots."

"So?" Charles said.

"You have to kick things like trees for years for that to happen," Hok said, "and you have to kick them *hard.* Also, look how battered and bruised his elbows are. He uses them a lot. He's even gone through the trouble of wrapping his hands with rope. I've never seen that done before, but I'll bet it protects and strengthens his hands while delivering maximum damage to his opponent."

"Rope on the hands?" Seh said. "Ouch."

"I see what you mean now," Charles said. "The Mauler is going to lose bad. He doesn't look like he practices at all."

"That's not entirely true," Hok said. "Look at the Mauler's ears. See how they look both puffy and rock-hard at the same time? Sort of like the vegetable *hua ye cai*—cauliflower? That comes from years of having your head banged against the ground. The Mauler is a wrestler."

"Wow," Charles said. "That's amazing. So, you still think the Assassin will win?"

Hok nodded. "It looks to me like he practices more."

A large gong sounded from somewhere near the betting table, and Hok watched the Siamese Assassin spring immediately into action. He raced toward the Mauler at full speed, leaping high into the air with a flying-knee attack.

The Mauler stood his ground and swatted the Assassin out of the air like he would a fruit fly.



The Siamese Assassin crashed to the ground.

The crowd roared with laughter, and Charles turned to Hok. "Are you sure about your choice?"

"Just watch," Hok replied.

Seemingly unfazed, the Assassin jumped to his feet and raised his roped hands in front of his face. He began to taunt the Mauler in a foreign language.

The Mauler scowled and took two lumbering steps toward the Assassin, crouching low as though he were going to attempt a wrestling takedown.

In the blink of an eye, the Assassin shot forward and delivered a vicious low kick with his shin to a band of particularly sensitive sinews on the outside of the Mauler's lead leg, just above the knee.

*CRACK!*

Hok felt the brutal impact just as much as she heard it. The crowd gasped, and the Mauler howled in pain.

"Somebody is going to feel *that* in the morning," Seh said.

Hok shook her head and watched as the Mauler lifted his damaged leg. As soon as he did, the Assassin shot forward a second time, repeating the technique on the Mauler's other leg.

*CRRRRACK!*

The second brutal kick echoed deep inside the pit and the crowd cringed as one, including Hok.

"Owwww," Charles said, rubbing his legs.

The Mauler teetered, and Hok watched the Siamese Assassin step in close, thrusting both rope-bound hands up toward the Mauler's towering head. Hok waited for the Assassin's fists to collide with the Mauler's face, but that didn't happen. Instead, the Assassin wrapped his hands around the back of the Mauler's head and pulled his opponent's face straight down while jumping up and thrusting his knee skyward. The Assassin's knee collided squarely with the Mauler's nose.

*CRUNCH!*

The sound filled the fight club, and the Mauler wilted in an awkward heap, unconscious.

The crowd went wild.

Several crowd members began to jump up and down, waving their wager sticks high over their heads, while others threw their wager sticks to the floor in disgust.

Ignoring the crowd, the Siamese Assassin dropped to his knees in front of his fallen opponent and bowed three times. Hok realized it was a sign of respect.

The pit door opened and the Assassin stood. Hok watched him walk out through the doorway. She noticed that he appeared to be walking into a dimly lit tunnel. He passed two men with *qiangs* who were obviously guards, and continued on until Hok couldn't see him anymore.

Hok continued to stare through the open doorway and saw a lone man approach from the depths of the tunnel. He wore a stained robe, long gloves, and a leper's shroud. The man strolled confidently into the pit without even acknowledging the guards and walked over to the Mongolian Mauler. He wasn't a big man, but he easily hoisted the large unconscious fighter over one shoulder and carried the Mauler back into the tunnel.

Hok realized that he was a one-man clean-up crew. He was probably dressed in that outfit to protect himself against blood, germs, and anything else that might rub off on him while he did his dirty work. Hok shivered. What a horrible job.

The crowd began to calm down, and LaoShu took the floor once more.

"How about that quick piece of handiwork?" LaoShu announced. "Or should I say, legwork? Ha ha! I guess big things really do come in small packages! If you enjoyed that matchup, wait until you see what we have in store for you now. This next competitor is not a criminal, but a promising up-and-comer who is fighting for a position within our esteemed Emperor's ranks. He is undefeated in the pit with a record of six wins and no losses, and tonight he is the favorite. This man is known for his fast hands and even faster feet. Always on the move and constantly on the attack, he's been known to skitter across the pit bricks like a drop of rainwater on a hot wok. Don't blink! You might miss the whole thing! Ladies and gentlemen, may I present the Kung Fu Crippler!"

Hok stared at the open pit doorway and saw a small, wiry man coming out from the depths of the tunnel. He raced round and round the pit in a tight circle, never slowing. His black hair was also cut very short, and he had a large bald spot on the top of his head. Sweat poured out of it like a fountain. The Kung Fu Crippler leaped to the very center of the pit floor and began a random combination of push-ups, squat thrusts, and shadowboxing punches.

The crowd went wild.

"What is he doing?" Charles asked.

"Wasting a lot of energy," Hok replied.

Seh smirked. "I don't even have to see him to know that that man is a fool. Do you know who he is fighting?"

"No," Charles said. "I didn't get to see the list."

"Let's hope it's Fu," Seh said.

"Why?" Charles asked.

"You'll see," Seh replied.

The crowd quieted down, and LaoShu spoke again. "I'd like to present to you now the challenger. He's a sizable chunk of fresh meat that we're going to serve up raw for the Kung Fu Crippler! He may be young, but my sources tell me he's tough. You all know the rules. The last one standing wins! Guards, bring in the prisoner!"

Hok stared into the tunnel and saw the two armed guards disappear into the darkness. A few moments later, they reappeared, prodding the challenger with their *qiangs*.

The crowd unleashed a series of boos and catcalls for the challenger, but they abruptly stopped once he came into full view. It was obvious that the crowd didn't know what to make of the man-child who stepped into the pit, snarling like a ferocious beast. Even the Kung Fu Crippler stopped and stared.

The challenger locked eyes with the Crippler and slowly began to stalk him.

"It's Fu, isn't it?" Seh asked.

"Yes," Hok replied. "I feel sorry for Mr. Crippler."

# CHAPTER 31

Hok watched as Fu stalked the Kung Fu Crippler near the center of the fight club pit. The Crippler began to jump around again, shadowboxing furiously to the delight of the crowd.

Hok rolled her eyes and looked over toward the bettors' table. A mob of people were wagering at a frenzied pace.

LaoShu cleared his throat and made an announcement. "Ladies and gentlemen, it seems there's been a huge interest in people betting on the Kung Fu Crippler now that we've seen his opponent. I will wait a few more moments before sounding the gong. Get those wagers in!"

Hok glanced down into the pit and saw that Fu

was now standing still as a statue while the Crippler continued his antics.

"Uh-oh, Seh," Hok said with a grin. "Fu is locking in on his target."

Seh chuckled.

"What's going on?" Charles asked. "Why do you two keep laughing?"

"Fu is going to eat the Crippler for dinner," Seh replied.

Charles eyes widened. "Really?"

"He's not literally going to eat him," Hok said. "Though it probably appears that way. Growing up, we had an instructor who looked and acted just like the Kung Fu Crippler. He even had a similar bald spot. We called him the Mosquito because he was small and always buzzing around. He never stood still. He taught hand boxing and believed the best way to fight was to constantly be moving. He said it made you a more difficult target. However, larger people like Fu often believe that moving all the time does nothing but waste energy. Fu hated sparring with that instructor. The instructor used to pick on Fu, buzzing around him and jabbing him with short punches, trying to get Fu to learn how to fight someone like him. Unfortunately for the instructor, Fu's training eventually paid off."

"What did he do?" Charles asked.

"Fu was only ten years old at the time," Seh replied, "but he managed to land a hard right hand to the instructor's jaw. The instructor didn't wake up for a week."

“That would have been something to see,” Charles said.

Seh nodded in the general direction of the pit. “I wish I could watch. It’s about to happen again.”

Charles scratched his head. “Seh, are you sure you don’t want to place any wagers tonight? I could go check the bettors’ table and see what the odds are. If you think Fu is definitely going to win—”

“No, Charles,” Seh said. “Now if you don’t mind, I want to listen to the bout.”

Charles frowned and slumped back into his chair.

LaoShu shouted, “All right, I can’t take the suspense anymore! Let the games begin!”

The gong sounded, and the crowd roared.

Hok watched as the Kung Fu Crippler continued his crazy shadowboxing, now moving steadily toward Fu.

Fu planted his feet shoulder-width apart and raised both his hands. He formed a tiger claw with his left and positioned it in front of his face. He formed a regular fist with his right and cocked it behind his ear.

Fu growled, and the Crippler chuckled.

“Well, hello to you, too, Kitten,” the Crippler said.

The crowed erupted into laughter, but Fu didn’t react. Hok knew that Fu had entered a trancelike state. Nothing would distract him now.

The Crippler moved forward to just beyond Fu’s reach, and his own reach as well. He began to throw crisp jabs at Fu’s head. The crowd went wild. Hok, however, could tell that the Crippler’s punches wouldn't connect. They were meant to test Fu's reflexes and see what sort of range Fu had. None of the punches were actually close enough to hit Fu.

It was obvious that Fu knew what the Crippler was up to. Fu remained perfectly still.

The crowd began to boo. They wanted to see Fu throw punches, too. A moment later, they got their wish.

The Crippler leaned forward and committed to a punch destined for Fu's temple. It was a looping overhand shot, and Fu could have seen it coming from a *li* away. He shifted his left forearm up to block the Crippler's right-hand punch, but it really wasn't necessary because his own straight right hand connected with the Crippler's chin first.



The Crippler's head snapped back so hard, his bald spot appeared to bounce off his spine. He spun once . . . twice . . . then fell to the floor, straight as a board, out cold.

The crowd sat silent for a moment, then exploded with a flurry of cheers, boos, and everything in between. Charles cheered so loud, Hok had to cover her ears. Seh even yelled out a few times.

Hok looked over toward the bettors' table and saw a scattering of men race up to it with bamboo sticks held over their heads like trophies. They must have bet on Fu. Most of the crowd members, however, broke their wager sticks over their knees and hurled them at the Crippler, who was still clearly unconscious on the pit's brick floor.

Hok glanced down at Fu and saw that he stood over the Crippler like a tiger over its kill, growling. At the Emperor's table, Hok could see that most of the group members were clearly disappointed, especially Tsung. HaMo, on the other hand, sat alone at his table, laughing so hard that his massive chins jiggled.

Hok looked back down into the pit and saw the two armed guards enter it from the tunnel doorway. They raised their *qiangs*, pointing them directly at Fu.

"Time to go back to your cage," one of the guards shouted. "Inside!"

Fu snarled, but did as ordered. He headed for the pit doorway.

"Seh!" Hok whispered. "They're taking Fu away!"

Seh laid one hand on his midsection. "Do you want to make our move?"

"No," Charles said in a surprisingly forceful tone. "There's nothing we can do. I might be able to take care of those two guards with my two *qiangs*, but the Emperor has ten armed soldiers directly across the pit from us. If I start shooting, so will they. We'll have to figure out a different way to rescue Fu."

Hok bit her lip. She knew that Charles was right. She watched Fu disappear into the tunnel.

"I wonder what that rat is up to," Charles said.

Hok followed Charles' gaze and saw LaoShu hurrying toward the main fight club entrance. Her eyes widened. In through the front door walked a petite woman dressed head to toe in black. The woman had long, luxurious hair that was nearly as long as that of her companion—a man with a thick ponytail braid so lengthy, he had the end of it tucked in his sash.

Hok turned to Seh. "Your mother just entered with Tonglong!" she whispered. "It looks like LaoShu is escorting them toward the Emperor's table."

Seh scowled. "I had a feeling they would show up. I'll keep my head down. It's not like I can see anything anyway."

Hok patted Seh's arm and saw his snake tense beneath his sleeve.

Hok turned to watch Tonglong and AnGangseh. They reached the Emperor's table and dropped to their knees, kowtowing. Hok couldn't see the Emperor's face clearly, but she got the impression he was pleased to see them. Specifically, he seemed to fixate on AnGangseh, who appeared to also have the attention of every man in the crowd.

Tonglong and AnGangseh stood, and attendants brought chairs for them to sit at the Emperor's table. LaoShu stepped to the pit's edge and made an announcement.

"Ladies and gentlemen, you are not going to believe who just joined us! Please help me in extending a hearty welcome to yet *another* former Fight Club Grand Champion—Tonglong, the Mantis!"

Tonglong bowed to the crowd, and the people responded with a rousing round of cheers and applause.

Hok glanced at Seh. He was grinding his teeth.

The crowd began to calm down, and LaoShu spoke.

"Let's get back to the action, shall we? How about that last bout? That kid sure packs a punch! It was over a little too quickly for my taste, though. Perhaps this next one will go a little longer and be a bit more . . . colorful. That color being blood-red, of course! Put your hands together for a battle-hardened veteran. He's returning to the pit for the tenth consecutive year to try his luck at the championship one last time. Because we'd all like to see him achieve his goal, we've given him a few pointers, so to speak. Scar!"

The crowd cheered and several people stood as a large man rushed through the tunnel doorway. Hok thought he looked to be close to forty years old. He had thick scars up and down his hairy arms, and a long thin one across his pimpled neck. His hair was tied up in some sort of knot, and he held a spear in each hand. In his yellow crooked teeth was a long knife.

"Look at all those weapons!" Charles said. "Are you sure you don't want to bet, Seh? I don't see how that guy can lose."

"You don't even know who his opponent is," Seh said. "Stop pestering me. Don't you have any money with you?"

"I do have a few coins," Charles said. "It's not much, but I suppose I could bet them—"

"You had better hurry up, then," Hok said.

Charles stood and raced over to the bettors' table.

Hok sighed and leaned toward Seh. "I don't understand why he is so excited about wagering."

Seh shrugged.

"Guards, bring in the challenger!" LaoShu shouted. "It's time for a little monkey business!"

Hok gripped Seh's arm and looked toward the pit doorway. She saw the two guards throw Malao through it. Normally, Malao would have landed in a tight tuck and roll. This time, however, he hit the brick floor like a tomato dropped from a treetop. The crowd roared with laughter.

"Was that Malao?" Seh said.

"Yes," Hok replied. "Something's wrong."

Hok watched Malao stand on wobbly knees and shake his head like he was trying to clear it. He looked around, wide-eyed. It was obvious that Malao had no idea where he was.

"Malao has been drugged!" Hok whispered. "I was in that same state of mind not too long ago. I recognize the signs. I would fade in and out of consciousness without warning. Malao won't be able to fight in that condition. We have to do something!"

"Are the two guards Charles mentioned still down there?" Seh asked.

"Yes—" Hok said.

"What about the soldiers?" Seh asked.

Hok glanced across the pit. "Still there."

Seh clenched his fists. "Unfortunately, there isn't anything we can do right now. Let's wait and see how Malao does."

"Seh," Hok said, "Malao's opponent is holding two spears and a dagger. His name is *Scar.* He's seen his share of blade fights. Malao is weaponless—"

"Unless you want to borrow Charles' *qiangs* and jump into the pit, I don't know what else we can do," Seh said. "Speaking of Charles, where is he?"

Hok glanced at the mob of people still crowded around the bettors' table. She couldn't see Charles.

"I don't know where he is," Hok said.

The gong sounded and Malao shrieked. Hok looked down in time to see Scar launch a spear at Malao.

Hok held her breath, then relaxed as Malao sprawled to the floor, narrowly avoiding the spear's glistening metal tip. Before he could get back up, though, Scar launched his other spear.

Malao shrieked again and rolled clumsily to one side. The second spear grazed his shoulder before rattling off the wall of the pit.

Malao howled and Hok saw a dark circle forming through his crimson robe.

"Malao is hurt!" Hok whispered to Seh. "Scar grazed his shoulder with a spear."

"He'll be okay," Seh said. "He's a clever fighter."

"If anything else happens to him," Hok said, "I'm going to help."

Seh didn't reply.

Hok watched Malao curl into a tight ball and begin to shiver, his eyes closed. The drugs definitely seemed to be controlling him.

Scar took the knife from his teeth and raised it up. He began to walk slowly toward Malao.

The crowd began to chant, "SCAR! SCAR! SCAR!"

Hok stood. Enough was enough. She didn't care about Tonglong or AnGangseh or Tsung or anyone else. She needed to help Malao. "STOP!" Hok cried.

But no one listened. Scar continued forward.

Seh grabbed at Hok's arms, but she shrugged him off. She adjusted the bag strap across her neck and over one shoulder and jumped onto the table, grabbing one of the drinking bowls. She hurled it at Scar, striking him on the crown of his head.

"LEAVE HIM ALONE!" Hok shouted, but the words and the bowl had no impact. Scar was unstoppable. He positioned himself over Malao's quivering body.

The crowd continued to chant, "SCAR! SCAR! SCAR!"

Scar thrust the dagger down, and Hok screamed.

Malao screamed, too—loud enough to make Scar flinch in mid-swing. At the same time, Malao's hand lashed out, ramming a splintered piece of bamboo wager stick he'd been hiding into the side of Scar's calf.

Scar cursed and his leg buckled, his knife swing going wide. Malao twisted out of the path of the tottering giant, but Hok watched in horror as Scar twisted in the same direction as Malao. Scar let himself drop to the ground, knees first, and slammed into the side of Malao's wobbly head. Malao was unconscious before he even hit the brick floor.

A few of the crowd members gasped, but most of them burst into cheers. They began to chant, "FINISH HIM! FINISH HIM! FINISH HIM!"

Hok stared into the pit, wide-eyed, as Scar planted his knees firmly on either side of Malao's limp head and rose up, hoisting his knife high.

"NOOOOO!" Hok cried, and she leaped into the pit, landing on the bricks in a tight single roll. She hopped to her feet, and her turban shifted over her eyes. Hok tore it off and screamed at Scar, "What's wrong with you, trying to kill a little boy? Can't you see that he's been drugged! Fight me! Leave him alone!"

Scar turned and stared at Hok, looking confused and angry. He lowered the knife and stood.

Scar took a step toward Hok, the broken bamboo stick still protruding from his calf.

"Stand down, Scar!" LaoShu yelled from above. "We'll count this as a victory for you! Guards, get that crazy girl out of there!"

The crowd began to boo, and someone shouted, "Scar didn't get to finish! We want a proper ending!"

People began to throw all sorts of items into the pit—drinking bowls, wager sticks, even food. Hok covered her head with her arms.

"Everyone, please calm down!" LaoShu shouted. "No need to get too excited. The outcome of this bout is clear. If you bet on Scar, you've won. No need to lose control!"

"LaoShu!" someone shouted. "I may be able to help. . . ."

Hok looked up to see that it was Tsung speaking. He turned to face the pit and stared straight at her.

"If these people want a proper ending," Tsung purred, "I'll give them one. Have the pit cleared out, but leave the girl to dance with me."

# CHAPTER 32

Hok looked away from Tsung and glanced up at LaoShu to see his reaction. LaoShu looked down at her, and his beady eyes widened.

"General Tsung!" LaoShu shouted. "Is that who I think it is?"

Tsung nodded, and LaoShu clapped his hands. Hok's heart began to race. She glanced at Tonglong and AnGangseh. They both started laughing.

Hok wanted to look over at Seh, but she knew it wouldn't do much good. He couldn't see her, and Charles was still off somewhere else. Instead, she looked back at LaoShu.

"Ladies and gentlemen!" LaoShu announced. "Did you just hear what I heard? Former Grand Champion

General Tsung is going to return to the pit! His opponent will be none other than Enemy of the State Number One! That girl in the pit may appear harmless, but looks can be deceiving. My sources tell me she is a superb fighter and personally responsible for the demise of the beloved Shaolin Temple. What do you think about that?"

The crowd began to boo, and someone shouted, "Kill her!"

LaoShu raised his hands. "Whoa! Not so fast. Wouldn't you like to wager on the outcome of this bout first? See the clerks at the bettors' table for details. You have until the sound of the gong to place your bets. Attendants, to your stations!"

The crowd jumped to its feet, and people began to rush frantically toward the bettors' table. Hok scanned the room and noticed an attendant running over to HaMo's table. HaMo dumped a huge bag of money on the table, and the attendant began to sift through it while counting out wager sticks.

Hok glanced quickly over at Seh. He sat alone, listening, and Charles still wasn't there.

Hok heard the pit door open and she turned to see the two armed guards standing beyond it. "Come on, Scar," one of the men said. "You heard LaoShu."

Scar scowled and glared at Hok, then threw something at her. It was the blood-soaked bamboo wager stick that had been in his calf. Hok jumped out of the way, and the stick clattered to the floor among the other refuse.

Scar limped through the doorway. As soon as he entered the tunnel, Hok saw the shrouded cleanup man coming from the other direction. The Cleaner shoved his way past Scar and headed for Malao.

The last thing Hok wanted was that filthy man touching her little brother. Who knows what kind of germs were crawling on him. She stepped between him and Malao, and one of the guards shouted, "Back up to the wall, girl! Let the man do his job."

Hok glanced at the pit entrance and saw the two guards beyond the doorway. They both were staring down their *qiang* barrels at her.

Hok gritted her teeth and backed up nearly to the wall. What had she gotten herself into?

The Cleaner hoisted Malao over his shoulder and left the pit. Two more men came out of the tunnel with brooms and quickly swept up the broken wager sticks and other debris, then left.

Hok looked up at LaoShu and he nodded to her, a huge pointy-toothed grin on his face.

"Let the games begin!" LaoShu announced, and the gong sounded.

Tsung stood, and the crowd roared.

Tonglong stood, too, placing a hand on Tsung's shoulder. They spoke for a moment, then both looked at Hok and grinned. Hok watched as Tonglong removed something from around his neck and gave it to Tsung, who then retied it around his own neck.

People began to chant, "LEOPARD MONK! LEOPARD MONK! LEOPARD MONK!"

Hok felt the walls, floor, and even the air around her vibrate from the crowd's chanting. Tsung jumped onto the top of the narrow metal railing in front of the Emperor's table and balanced there for several moments. Hok watched him tense every muscle in his body until he, too, began to vibrate.

With a vicious snarl, Tsung hurled himself into the pit, somersaulting twice before landing on the pit's brick floor in a flawless single roll. The cheers of the crowd were deafening as General Tsung popped onto his feet and turned to face Hok.

"So, we meet again?" Tsung purred. "Welcome to my home away from home. I missed you after our little encounter at the prison."

Hok's eyes narrowed. She took a step back, and the crowd began to boo.

"Tell me, what do you think of the present Tonglong just gave me?" Tsung asked. He reached into the collar of his robe and pulled out a tiny green object on a silk thread. It was her jade crane!

Hok took a step toward him, then stopped. What was she thinking?

After her step forward, the crowd began to cheer again.

"Make the crowd happy," Tsung said. "Give the people what they want. Come and get your trinket."

Hok didn't know what to do. She started to glance up at Seh, then thought better of it.

Tsung must have been following her eyes. He looked up at Seh, then back at her.

"We've been watching you and the other two since

you first stepped into the fight club entrance line hours ago," Tsung said. "What do you take us for, fools?"

Hok's heart sank. She should have known better.

"We already have the round eye," Tsung purred. "It was stupid of him to go to the bettors' table alone."

Hok's mouth dropped open.

"The boy up there with the silly hat is your brother Seh, isn't he?" Tsung asked. "I remember him from an encounter outside the walls of the destroyed Shaolin Temple. I suggest you say goodbye to him now. Like you and the round eye, he will not be leaving here alive."

Hok twitched. She risked a glance up at Seh, and Tsung lunged at her throat.

Hok was ready. She had a feeling Tsung was trying to distract her. She hopped to one side, flattening herself against the pit's circular wall. Tsung leaped straight past, narrowly missing her. Hok knew he wouldn't miss again. She needed a plan to fight a leopard on the ground.

With her back still to the wall, Hok felt the coarse, irregular bricks digging into her shoulder blades. She got an idea.

Hok glanced across the pit and ran as fast as she could toward the two guards watching the action from the tunnel entrance. The guards scrambled to close the door. Hok had no intention of attempting to run into the tunnel; she simply wanted Tsung to think that was her intention and follow her.

Tsung did follow her, with amazing speed.

As Hok reached the tunnel door, it closed completely. Still running full speed, she veered to the right and jumped into the air, straight at the rough bricks surrounding the doorway. Hok stuck her right foot out in front of her, curled back her toes, and hit the irregular wall at full speed with that single foot. She bent her right knee to absorb the energy of the impact, then released the energy back toward the wall by straightening her leg like a tightly coiled spring. Hok sailed backward high into the air with her arms spread wide, while Tsung was still coming toward her, low to the ground.

Hok twisted around in mid-air and lashed out with a bony elbow. It connected with Tsung's forehead, directly over his left eyebrow. This was the exact spot Hok was aiming for. She knew that a person's face is rich with numerous blood vessels that pass between thick-boned skull and parchment-thin skin. Her powerful blow split the skin wide open. Blood poured into Tsung's eye, making it impossible to see out of.

One eye down, one to go. Hok floated to the ground beyond Tsung and turned to face him.

Tsung wiped his brow with his sleeve, but it made no difference. Before he could blink twice, his eye was flooded with crimson again.

Tsung roared. So did the crowd. Some of them cheered, while others booed.

Hok chanced a glance in Seh's direction and saw that he was hunched over, facing the lowest rung on the railing. The bulge around his midsection had disappeared. Seh was securing the rope to the bottom of the railing!

Hok glanced back at Tsung, and Tsung sprang.

Hok scuttled sideways, narrowly avoiding Tsung's grasp. She zigged and zagged her way to the opposite side of the circular pit, and when she reached the far wall she went airborne again. This time, she hit the irregular bricks with her left foot and attempted the same maneuver, twisting in mid-air.

Tsung didn't fall for it again. As Hok swung her elbow at his other eye, Tsung reached up and took hold of Hok's arm, pulling her from the sky.

Hok maintained her balance and managed to hit the ground feetfirst. She threw herself powerfully to the ground and her arm slipped free of Tsung's grasp.

Before Tsung could pounce on her, Hok hopped back to her feet and scurried across the pit once again. She realized that Tsung hadn't managed to lock on to her arm, which meant that he might be having trouble with his depth perception. She knew that poor depth perception often came with seeing with only one eye. That gave her another idea.

When Hok reached the pit wall, Tsung was on her heels. She leaped at the wall as she had twice already, except this time she hit the bricks with two feet and redirected her energy into a powerful backflip high over Tsung's head. Hok formed crane-beak fists with both hands and thrust them at Tsung's right eyebrow.

Tsung managed to block Hok's right arm with a lightning-quick swing of his leopard fists. He swung at Hok's left arm and hit it, too, but it was a glancing blow.

Hok's crane-beak fist continued toward Tsung's face. Instead of striking Tsung's eyebrow as Hok had planned, though, the bunched-up tips of her four fingers and thumb sank into Tsung's right eye.

Tsung screamed.

Hok completed her flip, landing hard on her knees. She stood and wiped her hand across her dress, and realized that the entire fight club had grown silent.

Tsung was clawing at his face, trying to wipe the blood out of his one good eye. He shouted to LaoShu, "I need to cage this bird! I can't see a thing. Bring on the Ring of Fire!"



LaoShu clapped his hands excitedly. "My pleasure!" he said. He looked toward the pit entrance door. "Tunnel guards, you know what to do!"

The crowd cheered wildly and began to chant, "FIRE! FIRE! FIRE!"

Hok had no idea what was going on. She watched Tsung walk to the very center of the pit and stand perfectly still. Waiting.

# CHAPTER 33

Hok scanned the pit, looking for signs of what was about to come. She saw none. She adjusted the strap of the silk bag still dangling across her torso and glanced up at Seh. He was scowling, his ear cocked in the direction of the Emperor's table.

Hok looked over at the Emperor's table and saw Tonglong staring at Seh. Several of the soldiers surrounding the Emperor and Xie were now standing and had their *qiangs* raised in Seh's direction.

Hok glanced at AnGangseh. AnGangseh puckered her full lips and blew Hok a long kiss, waving goodbye.

Hok heard the pit entrance door open, and she turned to see a young man holding a large bronze cauldron. Applause filled the fight club. Hok barely heard him yell at her, "Move away from the wall!"

Hok glanced beyond the young man, into the tunnel, and saw the two guards. Their *qiangs* were aimed straight at her. She decided to do as she was told. She walked toward Tsung, cautiously.

"I won't attack you yet," Tsung said to her, trying to keep the blood pouring down his brow from running into his good eye. "It will be much more fun once the heat gets turned up."

The young man with the cauldron entered the pit, and the crowd's applause grew. Hok realized that they were cheering as much for the man as for what he was about to do.

The crowd began to chant, "GOLDEN DRAGON! GOLDEN DRAGON! GOLDEN DRAGON!"

Hok locked eyes with the young man and realized immediately that it was indeed her brother Long. He didn't acknowledge her, though. His face was expressionless.

Hok watched as Long began to ceremoniously pour what appeared to be lamp oil in a tight circle around her and Tsung. When Long had finished, he handed the empty cauldron to one of the guards just inside the tunnel, then turned and ran full-speed across the pit. When he reached the far wall, Long did as Hok had done and used the irregular bricks and his momentum to send himself high into the air. Instead of twisting around and throwing an elbow, though, Long reached up and grabbed one of the burning pit torches. He snapped it free and returned to the ground, landing softly on his feet with the torch in one hand.

The crowd burst into thunderous applause.

Long raised the torch high, and the crowd quickly quieted down. He approached the ring of oil and spoke softly to Hok. "The oil burns fast and furious, just like your opponent. You would be wise to avoid the flames. Better to fly into the jaws of the leopard than retreat and roast like a banquet pheasant."

"Those words are most insightful, Golden Dragon," Tsung growled as he whisked fistfuls of blood from his face. "How generous of you."

Long didn't reply. Still expressionless, he lowered the torch over the oil.

"Not so fast!" Tsung said. "You've given me an idea."

Long lifted the torch, and Tsung raised his one good eye toward the crowd, "Who wants to see me clip this criminal's wings?"

The crowd roared with applause and began to chant, "CLAW! CLAW! CLAW!"

Hok saw a large flash of silver from the direction of the Emperor's table and heard a loud *CLANG!* as something metallic hit the pit floor. Tsung bent down and picked the object up. Hok had no idea what it was.

"Hey, LaoShu!" someone shouted. "Unfair! I bet good money on this bout, and you're changing the tables by allowing a weapon after the gong. I demand equalization!"

Hok glanced up and saw that the speaker was HaMo. He had come down to the pit's edge, near the Emperor's table.

"What do you have in mind as an equalizer?" LaoShu asked.

HaMo reached into his robe and pulled something out. "This!" he said.

The crowd members closest to HaMo roared with laugher.

LaoShu chuckled and said, "Sure, HaMo. If you insist."

HaMo leaned over the railing and yelled down to Hok, "Catch!" He threw something that looked like the wooden handle of a short weapon. Hok reached up and caught the spinning object. It was Malao's carved Monkey Stick.

Hok gripped one end of the Monkey Stick and looked at Tsung. He was adjusting the strange object over his right hand. She could now see that it was a fingerless glove that had four long daggers attached to the back. The daggers began at the glove's sleeve and ran across the back of the hand, over the knuckles, and well beyond the length of the fingers.

The crowd continued to chant, "CLAW! CLAW! CLAW!"

Hok glanced up at Seh. He was on the edge of his seat, one ear now cocked in her direction.

Out of the corner of her eye, Hok saw Long lower

the torch. The oil ignited with a tremendous *WHOOSH!*

Hok closed her eyes against the intense heat and glare generated by a wall of flames that roared to her waist. She squinted in Tsung's direction and saw that he was still fumbling with his clawed glove.

HaMo yelled from above, "What are you waiting for, girl? Hit him!"

Hok took the hint. She swung the Monkey Stick as hard as she could at Tsung's right hand, but Tsung was too fast. He pulled his hand back, lashing out with the claw.

Hok hopped backward, out of harm's way. However, she landed dangerously close to the circular wall of fire. It lapped at her, waist high, and she was forced to step forward. The silk bag bounced off her stomach and she shoved it around behind her.

Tsung raised the claw up again, and Hok dropped to the ground, rolling to the opposite side of the burning circle of fire. She stayed on her knees and slipped one end of the Monkey Stick into her cupped palm, turning the stick downward so that the length of it was positioned along the inside of her forearm. She found that it stretched from the center of her hand to just beyond her elbow. Perfect.

Tsung rushed toward her, swinging the claw straight down at her head. Hok raised her forearm up and rotated it so that the claw connected with the wooden Monkey Stick. The daggers sank deep into the wood, but her arm was fine.

Still on her knees, Hok swung her free hand toward Tsung's lead leg and connected with a crane-beak fist. It sunk deep into a pressure point located on the outside of Tsung's leg, just above his knee. It was the same spot the Siamese Assassin had attacked with kicks.

Tsung snarled and his leg buckled, but he didn't go down. Hok tried to yank the Monkey Stick free of the daggers, but Tsung wrenched his arm back and Hok felt the Monkey Stick slip out of her hand. Tsung yanked the Monkey Stick off his claw and hurled it across the pit.

Hok took a step back, and the crowd gasped. Hok felt heat and glanced down to see that her silk bag had caught fire.



Hok tore her bag off in a frenzy, whipping it around in front of her by the strap. Tsung lunged forward and swung wildly at Hok with the claw, blinded by blood streaming from his brow. The very tips of the sharp claw daggers connected with the flaming bag, and bits of dried herbs flew out of slices in the bag. The bits caught fire, raining down on Tsung's head, neck, and shoulders.

Tsung cried out and raised his hands to protect his bloody face, and Hok threw the bag upward and away with all her might. She ignored the few flaming herbs that singed her own bare arms and head and lowered her bony shoulder, driving it as hard as she could into Tsung's chest.

Tsung stumbled backward, and Hok stayed with

him. She swept his flailing legs out from under him and grabbed at the jade crane around his neck, catching it in her hand. She snapped it free and leaped backward.

Tsung hit the brick floor with a blood-curdling scream. Hok shrieked in surprise as Tsung's entire silk uniform went up in flames. Tsung writhed and twisted, then fell still.

Hok listened for the crowd's reaction, expecting a chorus of boos. Instead, she heard someone shout, "FIRE! THE CLUB IS ON FIRE!"

Hok looked up to see smoke rising on one side of the pit. Brilliant yellow flames first licked two tables, then three, then four in rapid succession.

"THE BAG IGNITED MY TABLECLOTH!" a man cried as he raced for the exit.

People throughout the fight club began to scream and scramble, and Hok swallowed hard as she quickly tied the jade crane's silk thread around her neck. She saw that the Ring of Fire flames circling her were still roaring strong. She would have to wait before she tried to save herself.

Hok glanced at Seh, and her thin eyebrows raised up. He was climbing down the rope!

"GET THE EMPEROR OUT OF HERE!" a soldier yelled from above, and Hok looked over to see the group at the Emperor's table scrambling up the tiered floor toward the side exit. Xie's towering shoulders led the way, and HaMo brought up the rear. On either side of the Emperor were Tonglong and AnGangseh. Hok saw Tonglong look back at Seh and scowl.

"You did this!" LaoShu screamed. "It's all your fault!"

Hok looked up to see LaoShu standing at the railing, pointing at her. His head turned and stopped at the sight of Seh climbing down the rope. LaoShu headed for Seh.

"Seh!" Hok shouted. "Hurry! LaoShu is coming after you!"

"How much farther to the end of the rope?" Seh asked.

"One more body-length," Hok shouted back. "The end of the rope is another two body-lengths from the floor."



"Right," Seh said. He slithered to the rope's end and dropped with a loud "Ooof!"

Hok looked up and saw LaoShu reach the rope. He began to shimmy down it.

"LaoShu is coming down the rope!" Hok shouted to Seh. "Get away! I'll be right there!"

Seh began to back up, and Hok looked at the fire around her. It was still too high to risk jumping over. She glanced quickly toward the exits and saw that the last of the crowd members were shoving their way outside. The fire up there had already reached the club walls, and the ornate tapestries were ablaze. Flames licked the long bolts of cloth all the way up to the wooden roof rafters, igniting them, too. The whole building would soon collapse.

“You’ve destroyed my beloved fight club!” LaoShu squealed in his high-pitched voice. “You’ve ruined me! You will not get out of here alive!”

LaoShu reached the end of the rope, and Hok saw him dig the toes of his shoes into irregularities in the pit wall. He shifted his weight to his legs and flung the rope skyward, then dropped to the pit floor.

Hok watched the rope sail up over the railing, landing across their table. The only way out for them now was the pit door, and it was more than likely locked. Hok looked at LaoShu and saw a large ring of keys looped through his sash. One of them was sure to open the door.

Hok took two small steps backward and decided she needed to act. She raced forward, leaping high over the remaining Ring of Fire. She felt heat on her feet and legs, but nothing ignited.

Hok hit the ground running and headed for Seh.

LaoShu began to rant and rave like a lunatic as he reached into the folds of his robe. “How dare you come into my club and do such a thing! I will teach you a lesson, girl! I will teach both of you!”

Hok reached Seh’s side and gripped his arm, ignoring the snake that slithered wildly beneath his sleeve. “Brace yourself!” she said.

“Brace yourself, indeed!” LaoShu replied. He pulled a short *qiang* out of his robe and began to walk toward them.

Hok glanced around quickly. She saw the pit door directly behind her and Malao’s Monkey Stick on the floor within easy reach. She grabbed the stick and tried the door, but as she had feared, it was locked.

LaoShu laughed and raised his *qiang*. "You're mine!"

Hok gripped the Monkey Stick. She knew it would be no match against a *qiang*, but she would have to try. If she attacked LaoShu first, he would shoot her and perhaps Seh would at least have a chance of getting out of there alive. She needed to tell Seh about the keys.

"Seh," she whispered, "LaoShu has a ring of—"

"Someone is coming," Seh interrupted.

"What—"

The pit door suddenly flew open, crashing into Hok and Seh. Hok righted herself and turned to the doorway. In it stood the shrouded Cleaner in his stained garb.

"Close that door, trash collector!" LaoShu shouted at the man. "Or you'll be next."

The Cleaner didn't budge. He removed his gloves and Hok saw that his fingernails were filed to sharp points.

LaoShu scowled and aimed his *qiang* at Hok.

"That idiot enjoys his job a little *too* much," LaoShu said. "But I suppose there is no harm in letting him have his fun with you after I am through. No one is really quite sure what he does with all the dead bodies he takes out of here."

LaoShu released a maniacal laugh, and Hok saw

his single outstretched finger begin to tighten beneath the *qiang.*

Out of the corner of her eye, Hok saw the Cleaner begin to move, too. The filthy man whipped his body powerfully left and then right, like a dragon. At the same time, he reached one hand into his robe sleeve and snapped his wrist outward so fast, Hok could barely see it.

The end of an extraordinarily long chain whip lashed out, its sharp weighted tip slicing into LaoShu's hand. LaoShu shrieked and dropped the *qiang,* and it hit the ground with a loud *BANG!*

"ARRRR!" LaoShu cried, falling over. Hok looked down and saw blood pouring from a large round hole in his ankle.

The chain whip began to circle overhead, and Seh said, "Ying! I can sense him! Where is he?"

"Over here," the Cleaner replied. He shook his head violently and the shroud drifted off, revealing a carved dragon's face. It was Ying, without question.

"You!" LaoShu shouted at Ying. "What are *you* doing back in my club?"

"I came to say goodbye," Ying hissed. He lashed out with the chain whip a second time, and the weighted tip wrapped itself around LaoShu's ring of keys. Ying yanked on the whip and the key ring tore free from LaoShu's sash, into Ying's hands. LaoShu's robe spilled open and Hok saw that he had another *qiang* strapped to his scrawny chest.

"Hurry," Ying snapped at Hok from the doorway. "Inside the tunnel. You're coming with me."

Hok hesitated. *Follow Ying?* she thought.

"Do it!" Ying said. "Before I slam this door closed on all three of you!"

Hok blinked and looked down at LaoShu. He was reaching for his second *qiang*.

Ying began to close the door.

"Come on," Hok said, and shoved Seh through the doorway.

Turn the page
for a preview
of the fifth book in
THE FIVE ANCESTORS . . .

# EAGLE!

## Henan Province, China

## 4348 – Year of the Tiger

## (1650 AD)

# Chapter 1

BANG!

Sixteen-year-old Ying shoved his former sister, Hok, to the ground with all his might. He saw her eyes widen as a *qiang* ball whistled over her head. Ying's carved face twisted into an angry scowl. How many times was he going to have to save her life tonight? He turned and slammed the door closed on the burning arena of the Jinan Fight Club.

Inside the club's main tunnel, Ying's eyes quickly adjusted to the orange-yellow glow of torches lining the stone-walled corridor. He glanced down at Hok and, next to her, Seh. Through the smoke drifting in from under the door, Ying saw that Hok held a tiny jade crane in one hand and Malao's carved monkey stick in the other. Both were trophies from her time in the pit arena.

In his own hands, Ying held his long chain whip and a ring of keys he'd just taken from LaoShu, the *qiang*-wielding fight-club owner.

LaoShu screamed suddenly on the other side of the door and Ying heard roof timbers crash down. The ground and walls shook, and Ying knew that LaoShu—the Rat—would give them no more trouble.

Ying spat and pivoted away from the door, ignoring the pain of cracked ribs and weeks-old bone bruises. The nagging injuries were his trophies, presented to him in prison by General Tsung almost a month before.

Ying wrapped his chain whip around his waist and groaned. He grabbed the collar of Hok's dress, yanking her to her feet.

"Move!" Ying hissed, pointing down the corridor. He looked at his former brother Seh. "You too."

Hok took a step forward, but Seh didn't react. He just stared at Ying, blank-faced.

*What is wrong with Seh?* Ying wondered. He reached out to slap some sense into him, but Hok grabbed his arm.

"Seh is blind," Hok said. "Not deaf. He had an accident."

"Blind?" Ying said. "Leave him, then."

Hok shook her head. "No."

Ying shrugged. "Suit yourself." He spun around and walked quickly down the tunnel corridor, the rough cotton robe of his Pit Cleaner's disguise chafing his beaten flesh.

"Ying, wait," Hok said. She took Seh by the arm and hurried after Ying.

Ying slowed for a moment, scanning the corridor. He saw no sign of guards ahead. They must have cleared out after the fire began.

Ying glanced back and saw Hok and Seh catching up. They looked like a pair of children whose dress-up tea party had ended in a fistfight. Hok's elegant silk dress was torn in several places and bloodstained from her fierce battle with General Tsung in the pit arena. Seh's simple gray robe was covered in dirt and splotches of who knows what else from rolling along the pit arena floor en route to this tunnel.

Ying began to walk again. Hok and Seh remained on his tail.

"Why are you helping us?" Hok soon asked in a low voice.

"You got me out of that prison back in Kaifeng," Ying replied. "I am returning the favor."

"You already met your end of our bargain," Hok said. "You gave me information that helped me find Malao."

Ying scoffed. "Maybe you would consider information an equal trade for someone's life, but I do not. My injuries were too great to have survived much longer there. You saved my life, and I am honor-bound to return the favor."

"But how did you know we would be here in Jinan, at the fight club?" Hok asked.

"I didn't come to Jinan looking for you," Ying replied. "I came looking for Tonglong. I have a score to settle with him, and he frequents the fight clubs. I saw you and Seh standing in line outside with the Round Eye. I assumed you were up to something, and also assumed you would fail. I saw this as an opportunity to repay my debt."

Ying rounded a corner. Ahead of him were rows of holding cells for prisoners who were scheduled to fight that night. All of the cells were empty, save two. Inside one sat Fu. Malao was in the other.

Fu roared when he saw Ying, but Malao began to shriek, "Ying! Ying!"

One of Malao's shoulders was bloodstained and he had a huge lump on the side of his head.

Ying ignored him.

"What are you doing here?" Malao asked. "Are those *keys* in your hand?"

Ying hurried past without acknowledging him. He picked up his pace.

"Ying, wait!" Malao wailed. "Come back!"

Ying glanced over his shoulder and saw Hok heading toward the cells with Seh.

"Hok! Hok!" Malao shrieked. "Help us!"

Fu roared again.

"Ying!" Hok said. "Please come back. Malao is hurt. We need those keys."

"Sorry," Ying said, turning away. "I need the keys for the exit door."

"Let them out first," Hok said.

"No," Ying said. "There are too many keys on this ring. By the time I figure out which ones will open their cells, we could be dead from smoke or something else. I won't risk it."

"I am not leaving here without Fu and Malao," Hok said.

"Then my debt has been repaid," Ying said. "Goodbye."

Ying rounded another corner and began to run. *Foolish children*, he thought. *Don't know when to cut their losses.*

Ying reached the end of the next passageway and came to a halt. The tunnel split in two directions. One way led to a set of stairs that went up to the fight club, while the other sloped gently upward toward a ground-level exit door. If he were to encounter any guards or others fleeing the burning fight club, this would be the place.

Ying squeezed the key ring tight so it wouldn't jingle, and peered around the corner. Smoke was streaming toward the exit. That meant the exit door was open, sucking the smoke toward it.

Ying listened closely.

Down the corridor in the direction of the exit, he heard footsteps. Someone coughed. "I can't believe we're being sent back in here," a man said. "We should just wait by the exit door. It's the only way out for those kids."

"I don't make the orders," another man replied. "I only follow them. The captain said to make a quick sweep of the tunnels, then get out of here. The sooner we finish, the sooner we can get some fresh air. Men, prepare your *qiangs*."

Ying noted the unmistakable *click!* of a *qiang* mechanism being engaged, then another, and another. He might be able to get past a single soldier with a *qiang*, but not three. Especially in his weakened state. Unfortunately, he needed help.

Ying silently ran back toward the others, cursing his terrible luck. As he neared the prisoner cells, he could hear Malao sobbing. He also heard Fu pounding furiously against the bars.

Hok saw Ying first. She opened her mouth to speak, but Ying cut her off. "There are at least three men coming this way with *qiangs*," he said. "They intend to finish us. If I release Fu and Malao, will you follow my orders?"

Fu growled, but Malao said, "I'll do it, Ying! I'll do whatever you say! I'm a little dizzy and my shoulder is sore, but I can still fight. Get me out of here!"

"Hush!" Ying said. "Keep your voice down." He stared hard at Fu. "What about you, Pussycat?"

Fu didn't reply.

Hok gave Fu an icy stare. "Be logical, Fu," she said. "There isn't much time."

"Fine," Fu grumbled, locking eyes with Ying.

Ying fought back a smirk. Fu was irritating and immature, but at least he was always ready for a fight. Fu would go first.

Ying flipped through the ring of keys, selected one, and stuck it into Malao's cell door. The door swung open.

"Hey!" Malao whined. "You said you didn't know which key would open this door."

"Lucky guess," Ying snapped. He walked over to Fu's cell and unlocked it. As the door swung open, Fu snarled in Ying's face and muscled past.

"After you, Pussycat," Ying said. "Put those feline instincts to use."

Fu rushed forward.

Ying started after Fu, and Hok handed the monkey stick to Malao. Malao grinned excitedly. "Where did you get this?"

"From HaMo while I was inside the fight club," Hok replied. "I'll tell you about it later. Are you sure you're okay?"

"I'm fine," Malao said. He and Hok followed with Seh in between them.

Fu soon stopped, and Ying watched Fu's head tilt to one side. Fu's low-light eyesight was excellent, but his ears were even better. Fu sank to his haunches and held up four fingers.

*Four guards,* Ying thought. *That's five against four. No problem.* He looked back at Hok, Seh, and Malao, and held up four fingers. Hok and Malao nodded back. Hok whispered the information into Seh's ear.

Ying sank to the ground and slipped the chain whip from around his waist. He gathered it up in one hand and shoved the key ring behind his sash. He slid over to Fu's side and mouthed five words: Angry Tiger Moves the Mountain.

Fu nodded once and compressed his body into a large ball. A heavy boot scraped the floor just ahead of them, and Fu sprang with a tremendous roar.

"Oooof!" the lead guard groaned as Fu slammed into his midsection. The guard's long *qiang* fired on impact with a characteristic *Click! . . . Fizz . . . BANG!,* the lead ball burying itself harmlessly in the wall of the tunnel. Fu hammered a tiger-claw fist into the man's jaw, silencing him.

"What's going on up there?" a guard called out.

No one offered a reply.

Ying eased his back against the tunnel's stone wall and saw the outline of a second guard creeping forward with his long *qiang* leveled at Fu's head.

"Crazy Monkey Swats the Fly!" Ying shouted,

and Malao responded by racing forward, swinging his monkey stick wildly. The guard saw Malao coming and shifted his arms to protect himself, but he was too slow. Malao leaped high into the air and brought the monkey stick down on the crown of the man's skull with a tremendous crack. The guard slumped to the ground, out cold, his finger still on the *qiang's* trigger.

*Click! . . . Fizz . . . BANG!*

The *qiang* fired, its firestone-tipped hammer igniting black powder. The lead ball shot forward and the unsupported weapon flew backward out of the unconscious man's hands. The *qiang* crashed against one wall of the tunnel, while the lead ball thudded into the opposite tunnel wall in a shower of debris.

*Two down, two to go,* Ying thought.

A third guard stepped up through thickening smoke and froze at the sight of his unconscious comrades being stood over by two children. Ying took advantage of the man's hesitation and lashed out with his chain whip. The whip's weighted end wrapped itself around the end of the guard's *qiang* several times. Ying yanked the barrel of the *qiang* down and sideways and shouted, "Monkey Takes the High Road, Tiger Takes the Low!"

Fu and Malao attacked as one. Fu threw his shoulders into the man's knees at the same moment Malao sprang into the air and slammed his heels into the man's cheekbones. The guard sailed backward, releasing his grip on the *qiang* in order to use his hands to break his fall. That proved to be unnecessary, as the fourth guard ended up breaking the third guard's fall for him.

Fu wrestled the *qiang* from the fourth guard's hands, and Malao put both guards to sleep with his monkey stick.

Ying unwrapped his chain whip from the end of the third guard's *qiang* and put the whip back around his waist. He pointed to the remaining unfired *qiang* Fu was holding and said, "Give that to me."

Fu growled and took a step back.

Hok gave Fu a cold glance. "Do it, Fu," she said.

Fu handed the *qiang* over.

Ying slung one of the *qiangs* over his shoulder and pulled the second one tight across his chest.

"Follow me," Ying hissed. "No matter what happens, do not stop walking."

"What are we going to—" Malao began.

"No questions!" Ying snapped. He turned and walked away. Behind him, he heard the others scramble and follow.

When Ying reached the bend where he'd first heard the guards, he turned the corner without breaking stride. The smoke was quite thick now, still flowing toward the exit door. Perfect. The exit door was still open. He would no longer need the keys.

Ying stopped and laid the key ring down, then quickly looked over the *qiangs*. The pans were full of powder and the flints were locked firmly in place at the end of the hammers. He could only hope that each had a lead ball rammed down its barrel.

Ying slung one of the *qiangs* across his back, raised the other to his shoulder, and headed for the exit door.

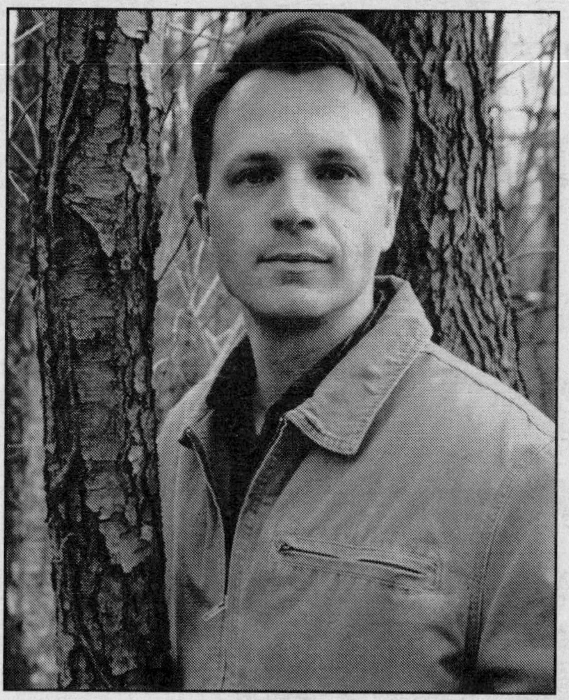

**Jeff Stone** lives in the Midwest with his wife and two children and practices the martial arts daily. He has worked as a photographer, an editor, a maintenance man, a technical writer, a ballroom dance instructor, a concert promoter, and a marketing director for companies that design schools, libraries, and skateboard parks. He recently traveled to the Shaolin Temple in China and while there passed his black-belt test in Shaolin-do kung fu.